AURA OF
DAWN

AURA OF DAWN

A DAUGHTER OF ZYANYA PREQUEL

MORGAN J. MUIR

Cover & book design by Morgan J. Muir
www.Morganjmuir.com
Cover Art by Tairelei
www.tairelei.com

Amazon ISBN: 9798599295778

For my parents
who always encouraged me.

Chapter 1

SPRING 1739 - MARACAIBO

MARIA STOOD in the fading evening light of the pier beside her father, a gentle breeze teasing her long black hair. The floating villages on Lake Maracaibo began to light their evening lights, and in the western distance, the nightly thunderstorm gathered. The three other young women chatted with each other, but Maria remained silent. Her heart lay heavy in her chest as she kept vigil over the body of her canine companion, friend, and protector.

Elisa had seen him first, just a squirming bundle of ears and paws in a sailor's rucksack. But it had been Maria who had claimed both the pup and his heart. Maria had saved his life, and he had saved hers in return.

As the darkness gathered, the other girls draped garlands over their lost playmate and returned to their homes. The funeral had been their idea. As soon as they realized the extent of Alistair's injuries, her three friends had spent the last few days cheerily making fanciful funeral plans. The romantic and untraditional idea of sending him off to sea enthralled them. Maria, however, had lain with her hound, draining herself of tears and doing all she could to ease his passing.

Maria watched the small barge move out onto the lake, backlit by the distant lightning. Nothing would ever bring joy to her again. Her gaze remained fixed on the dark smudge. It danced along the surface of the water until she lost it among the twinkling lights of the native's floating homes. The lights seemed to watch her, their sympathy at her loss nearly as painful as her guilt. Her eyes blurred as she watched. She struggled to blink back the tears, but they ran down her face anyway. She jumped when her father rested his hand on her shoulder, and she wiped away the wetness from her cheeks before turning toward him. For a moment, looking up into his face, Maria saw a depth in this man that went beyond just being her father.

The profound pain of loss that ached in her heart, loss of her dearest friend and confidant, she found reflected in his face. She knew, however, that his pain ran far deeper. He looked with unfocused eyes over the water. Perhaps he met the eyes of the natives who had come out to the edge of their *palafitos*, their floating village, to watch the strange ceremony. Perhaps he saw the ghost of her mother, whom Maria had never known, her loss still so fresh and painful that he never spoke of her to his daughter. What life had her father, Don Ciro Álvarez Bosque, merchant and businessman, lived and known that Maria knew nothing of? For the first time in her sixteen years of life, Maria wondered who her father truly was.

6

She turned back to the water, hoping to again find the barge among the broken reflection of the waning moon. But it was no longer there. The two of them remained in silence, each consumed with their own thoughts in the inky darkness.

***

The moon glistened across the calm waves of the lake, its light blurred by the clouds as Michael walked beside the ship's rail. The texture of the hard wood flowed beneath his fingers like frozen waves, guiding his fingers along inevitable paths. Michael looked up from the water, with its floating lights, to the stern of the anchored merchant ship. The floating wooden beast had been his home for the past several months as they'd crossed the world. He snorted at the thought. It wasn't home; it was merely a place to exist. The abandoned helm called to him. He was meant to have captained a ship like this, a path that had lain before him as frozen and inevitable as the wood grain of the rail.

Or so he'd thought.

A warm breeze full of floral scents blew across the deck. It reminded him forcibly of old, vague memories full of warmth and honesty. Scowling, he pulled his gaze from the helm and crossed to the other side of the deck. He ought to turn in for the night. The morning would bring the typical hectic rush of work, offloading and reloading merchandise. Just another day of backbreaking labor, and then he'd be back to the sea.

The ocean called to him, as she did to every sailor. Entrancing, fickle. Beautiful and dangerous. She promised the freedom of salty wind in his face while under full sail, and the heady exhilaration of struggling for his ship's life along with his own whenever she felt tempestuous.

Michael snorted, leaning against the rail. Her promises were as empty and unfulfilling as her threats were full. He was just a toy for her to use for her own amusement, to be tossed aside when she was done. Not unlike certain captains.

Below him on the dock, movement caught his eye. He watched a small group of young women, gathered at the edge of a nearby pier, throw things onto a small barge. It had all the air of a funeral, but a shockingly small one. The barge was pushed out and Michael watched it pass his ship by. That would be his end. Serving this ship, or another like it, until the sea claimed him for her own.

Michael slammed his fist into the rail. He belonged to no one. Not this ship. Not the sea. Not his father's name.

The breeze again flowed over him, pulling at his dark hair. Tucking his loose hair back behind his ear, he turned away from the water. He needed to gather his things and get some sleep. It was time, and this place would be as good as any.

***

The smell of the water, full of life and potential, drifted over Maria. The noise and bustle of the marketplace in the morning, punctuated by the cries of gulls in search of breakfast, were of little consequence as she moved toward the lake. Her friends followed behind her, their *duenna* trailing along some distance away, and Maria listened to them with only half an ear.

"Did we have to come this way?" Selena asked with a sigh as she picked her way through the muddy, busy street.

"There was no reason not to," Betania said with her usual conciliatory manner.

"Except that you thought it a bad idea," Elisa pointed out. "And it would take longer. And—"

"Oh hush," Betania said to her sister. "I thought it might be nice, and Maria wanted to come this way."

"Nice," Elisa muttered. "If you like the smell of fish guts." She swung her skirt to the side at the last minute to avoid brushing against a fishmonger's cart.

"You *would* think it's nice, Elisa," Maria cut in, annoyed by Elisa's persistent whining. She would never understand why Betania's younger sister *always* had to follow along. "We all know it's your favorite perfume, but you could really learn to be more judicious about it."

Selena laughed, and Maria knew Betania would be holding back her own laughter. Elisa would fume about it for a while and then try to come up with some cutting retort. The girl had actually begun to develop some real wit.

Not even a spark of amusement found its way into Maria as they moved through the patchwork of sunlight and shadows. While Maria's mind knew she should care—about something, anything—her soul simply didn't. She walked on, ignoring the chatter of her friends, and made her way to the pier. The glitter of the sun on the waves was the only thing bright; all else was muted. Dull.

The three other girls milled around her for a minute, forced by Betania to give her some time.

Elisa said something in a giggling whisper that Maria didn't care enough to hear. Betania nudged Maria out of her reverie and gestured discreetly to a young man walking down a nearby gangplank. He was tall, with dark hair, well dressed even if his clothes were a bit tattered, and he held a rucksack thrown over his shoulder. He looked out at the world with his head high and a grin, as if expecting something wonderful.

Maria scowled. How could anyone be so cheery?

"Come on," she said, a flare of anger overcoming her apathy and spurring her into recklessness. Lifting her head, she led the girls deliberately toward him.

"What are you doing?" Betania whispered urgently. Poor, quiet Betania, always trying to take responsibility but too timid to succeed. Maria took her arm firmly, and Betania fell into step.

"Seeing if Elisa can catch herself another salty puppy," Maria said, just loud enough for the other two to hear.

Elisa and Selena stifled giggles, and Betania tightened her grip on Maria's arm in disapproval but didn't try to stop her. Despite Maria's efforts to not look as they passed, she couldn't help but notice the young sailor's gaze following them.

"Pardon me, señoritas," he called out, not even trying to hide his British accent.

Maria grinned as she stopped the group.

"My name is Michael, and I'd be pleased to make the acquaintance of such lovely young women."

"He's all yours, Elisa," Maria said, and the four of them turned back towards the sailor.

Elisa stepped forward with her hand outstretched, a sickeningly charming smile on her face and her golden hair shining in the sunlight. "I'm Elisa Díaz Palomo, daughter of Don Sergio Díaz Montejo, Señor de la Cuesta."

Elisa paused just long enough for the young man to take her hand and shake it. "This is my sister, Betania, my cousin, Selena Abano Palomo, and our dear friend, Maria Álvarez Cordova." The girls curtsied as they were introduced, Betania and Selena both keeping their eyes modestly downward. "Welcome to Maracaibo, Miguel."

"Miguel. I like that." He released Elisa's hand and grinned. "*Merci*. It's not every day you're welcomed ashore by such visions of beauty. Might I walk with you for a bit, as we seem to be headed in the same direction?"

"What, away from the ship?" Maria whispered to Betania, who stifled a laugh with a demure cough and a gloved hand, still pointedly studying the muddy road.

Elisa looked Miguel up and down, then cast a glance at her older sister, whose grip dug into Maria's arm. Maria shrugged, and Elisa held out her elbow for Miguel. "Certainly. We would be delighted!"

"Here," Maria said, shifting Betania's death grip to Selena's arm as the group began forward. Shaking some feeling back into her own arm, Maria slowed to look back at the lake. The water glimmered beyond the waiting ships, whispering beneath the cacophony of life about … something. It urged her aching heart to come to it. But her father had insisted that she get through today, and so she would. With regret, she turned from the water and caught up to her friends.

How much trouble might she get in for this bit of brashness? Her father would probably laugh, though Doña Olivia would tighten her lips and use that disapproving tone. She could practically hear it now. *How dare you introduce yourself to some strange man! And a sailor at that. Surely you have better manners and care for your person. Blah blah blah.*

Maria wrinkled her nose at the imaginary lecture. It wasn't as though they were in any real danger. The girls always had an escort, be it the Díaz girls' duenna—who currently looked as though she'd bitten into a lemon— or a member of the house staff. Especially now that Alistair was gone.

Maria's throat tightened, and that stinging behind her eyes returned. She cut off that line of thought viciously, slamming the door shut on her melancholy. She wouldn't cry in public. Instead, she looked over Elisa's newest acquisition, determined to focus on something else. Anything else.

Miguel looked to be a couple years older than Maria, seventeen or eighteen perhaps, tall and well built. Life at sea appeared to have treated him well; he had a healthy color and moved gracefully. For a moment, she wondered about his teeth; she hadn't noticed them before. But then again, it wasn't as though she was buying a horse. Maria noted that he wasn't as broad as most men she had fancied, but he certainly wasn't bad to look at. If he was as young as she suspected, he would likely fill out in a couple more years, or so Nana always claimed of the young men her age.

He had dark hair, nearly as black as her own, which he wore pulled into a neat queue, tied at the nape of his neck. The loose sleeves of his white shirt billowed in the breeze and Maria imagined his arms would be nicely muscled. His boots, though well made, were worn, as was his faded waistcoat. Given his build, apparent health, and fine-though-worn apparel, the chances were good he wasn't just a deckhand. Perhaps a junior officer? Maria allowed herself a small grin as she imagined him fighting off pirates with the cutlass that swung at his hip.

Maria listened for a moment to Selena and Betania's conversation. They were going on about the number of ships in the busy harbor and the weather out in the Gulf of Venezuela beyond the lake. They'd obviously spent too much time listening to their fathers go on about business. Not interested in that tedious topic—she got enough of it from her own father—she moved forward to walk beside Miguel. Looping his bag over his shoulder to free his unoccupied arm, he offered Maria his elbow. Ignoring a moment of unease—this man was a stranger after all—she took his arm. He gave her a broad smile, and she smiled back at him, not caring that it didn't reach her eyes. Elisa shot her a withering look, which almost made Maria's smile genuine.

"Miguel and I were just talking about where he is from," Elisa said with a careless flip of her golden hair.

"Actually—Maria is it?—I was avoiding the subject of where I am from." He winked at her.

Maria rolled her eyes. "It's obvious from your accent that you're British, though your Castilian seems decent. You've also employed a smattering of French, so I'm sure you've dealt with them as well."

"And what would you conclude from that?" he asked.

"I'm willing to bet that you've travelled the world. So tell us, mighty traveler, what have you seen?"

Miguel slowed to a stop, and she could practically feel Elisa's chagrin as he looked at Maria. Maria turned to him, and their eyes met, his green eyes capturing her.

14

A few seconds, or perhaps an eternity, later Miguel broke contact, and they began forward again.

"Well," he began slowly, not looking at either of them, "I'm not really sure where I was born; somewhere in England, I'm told. My first memories are of being on a ship with my father, large as life, before me. I suppose I've travelled the world; it certainly feels like it. The last several years, I've mostly sailed the waters of Britain, France, and Spain. I have made the trip to India and back once. My father once told me that I'd even seen the Orient, though I don't really remember it."

While Elisa gave him her rapt attention, Maria opted to look him over more closely, as much as she could without being obvious. He had a finely shaped face, with lively eyes lined with dark lashes, and a very expressive mouth. He looked like the type of person who enjoyed laughing. *No,* she thought to herself, *Elisa can have him.*

"Anyhow," Miguel continued, "after finally coming to the New World, I think I've had just about enough traveling. Perhaps I'll stay on for a while, especially if life here is as sweet as the señoritas."

Elisa and Maria both blushed, but Maria regained her tongue first.

"If you are going to stay here you're going to need more of a name than just Miguel," Maria said.

"What's wrong with Miguel?" Elisa demanded, swinging forward to glare at Maria.

"Yes, please enlighten me, fair lady." Miguel disentangled himself from Elisa and gave Maria a mock bow. "What is wrong with my name?

Maria laughed lightly. "Nothing. I think Miguel is a fine name. You just seem to have misplaced your surname."

"Drat. I knew I left something on that ship." Miguel feigned consternation. "Should I go back and fetch it?"

"Perhaps if you just called to it, it would come." Elisa joined in the play and rethreaded her arm through his.

"Hmmm … It may be surly about being left behind. Perhaps if you angels attempted to call it."

Giggling, Elisa said, "Blanco!"

At the same moment, Maria spoke up with "del Mar."

"Whoa, señoritas, one at a time, please! Let's see, Elisa suggests Blanco, and Maria gives del Mar. What fine names for a man like me." He rolled his shoulders as though trying on a new coat. "They seem comfortable enough. I shall keep them both."

Elisa giggled yet again, and Maria just shook her head at the silliness. The warehouses had given way to the two-storied buildings of rock and stucco. A crossroads marked the edge of town, beyond which the buildings sat further apart, their boundaries marked by fences and the occasional palm tree. Miguel stopped, bowing again to the girls.

"Well, ladies, I'm afraid this is where we must part."

"I hope to see you again soon." Elisa batted her eyes at him, and Maria groaned. The girl was only fourteen, and was about as subtle as a brick to the head.

"I would like that very much. Casa de la Cuesta, right? I will surely call on you there." Miguel gave Elisa a most charming smile, too charming for Maria, but Elisa soaked it in. "In fact, I look forward to seeing all of you again." He shook each of their hands in turn. "Elisa, Betania, Selena. Maria."

Miguel held on to Maria's hand a moment longer than the others'. In a quiet voice meant only for her, Miguel added, "Especially you, Maria."

The other three girls started down the road while Maria stood there in a sort of shock, heat rising into her face. No one had ever been so forward with her before. He gave her a sheepish grin, breaking the spell, and she turned away to catch up with her friends. As they strolled away, a gaggle of gossiping, giggling geese, Maria looked back to see Miguel still standing where they'd left him, looking thoughtful.

"Miguel!" she called back as a mischievous feeling stole over her. He looked up and she continued, "Miguel, there's a merchant's office in town, just around the corner. There's pink coxcomb under the windows. You can't miss it. If someone were looking for employ, he might start there."

"I'll keep that in mind," he called back, raising his hand in farewell. *"Gracias!"*

She hurried back to her friends, looking back just before passing around a bend in the road. He still stood as they had left him. Finally, he hoisted his pack and turned back the way they had come.

Chapter 2

MARIA KEPT her eyes on her embroidery, her tension hoop held lightly against her leg. Betania sat beside her, sharing the second-best couch in the Casa de la Cuesta. Maria had spent so much of her childhood here, receiving her education with Doña Olivia's girls, that it nearly felt like home. Except that Casa de la Cuesta was far larger than the estate Maria shared with her father. One could get lost in the long pale halls here, in their cold grandeur. Her father's *hacienda* was far more welcoming.

Elisa had spread herself out on the best couch, of course, and Selena shared a seat with her aunt, Doña Olivia. "Well?" she asked, unable to contain herself any longer. "What did you think of him?"

"Think of whom?" Doña Olivia asked, as if she hadn't already interrogated both their duenna and the serving man who'd followed them.

"We were returning home, walking past the docks," Selena said.

"What on Earth were you doing there?" Doña Olivia's exasperated tone made Maria smile.

"Maria wanted to," Betania said quietly. "And I thought it would be best—"

"Maria wanted to, so you did." Doña Olivia cut her daughter off. "Honestly, child, when are you going to learn to make decisions for yourself?"

Maria looked up to see Betania quietly return her gaze to her embroidery.

"Regardless of how we got there, Tía Olivia," Selena continued, preventing the awkward silence from growing, "a young man asked if he could walk with us."

"I saw him first," Elisa cut in.

"Of course she did," Betania muttered under her breath to Maria, who smiled.

"He was disembarking a ship recently come in," Elisa said.

"He definitely wasn't disembarking a whale," Maria returned quietly to Betania.

"Certainly there is more to tell about him than that?" Doña Olivia prodded, her disapproval softening.

"Well …." Elisa straightened her back, looking down her nose at her embroidery. "He's lived his whole life at sea. He's been all around the world. India, the Orient and all over Europe, but this is his first time to the New World. He says it's the most beautiful place he's ever been, and that he's going to stay here for a while."

"Indeed?" Doña Olivia raised a perfectly shaped eyebrow.

Maria knew what would come next; the obligatory word of warning, lest Olivia's youngest daughter let her heart be snared and stolen away by a sailor.

"Be sure not to expect too much of him." Doña Olivia said. Maria could almost mouth the words along with her. "*Marineros* don't often stay at port for very long. Even when they try, it just doesn't last. When the sea is in their blood, it calls to them, beckons them home. For them, there is no resisting that siren's call." Doña Olivia's eyes rested on Selena, whom everyone claimed looked more like her mother, Natalia—Doña Olivia's sister—every day.

Maria waited for the inevitable comment about Selena's father, Don Vasco, being a good-for-nothing sea dog who had seduced Selena's mother, but it didn't come. As the room fell into silence, Selena didn't look up from her perfect, even stitches. Perhaps they should have been more alike, both losing mothers they couldn't remember, but Maria never had siblings whereas Selena's had died. But did that really matter if Selena couldn't remember them? No, the biggest difference between them lay in the fact that Maria had a father who cared. A father who, when things were hard, had stayed instead of running away and abandoning her to relatives, checking in on her only when his ship returned to Maracaibo. She couldn't imagine a world where her father, the indomitable Don Ciro Álvarez, larger than life and capable of solving any problem, was not there for her.

Selena again broke the silence, her voice level. "To answer your question, Tía Olivia, he's rather tall, taller than any of us, and his hair is dark like Maria's, but shorter, of course. I didn't get a good look at his eyes …."

"They're green," Maria offered.

"And he wore a cutlass," Elisa cut in, oblivious to the undertones of the conversation. "Oh, he looked so dashing!"

With the mood broken, the gossip continued on a lighter tone, and Maria fell out of the conversation. The fine cloth between her fingers was soft, but not nearly as soft as Alistair's ears had been. His ears had been his only soft part. The rest of his fur had been short and wiry, and her fingers ached to touch that rough fur again. Or to hear his bark as he rushed at her after they'd been parted, and to feel his bulk try to knock her down. She would laugh and wrestle with him, her best friend and faithful companion. But now, only emptiness awaited her, compounded by the knowledge that it was of her own making. She hadn't shed a tear for him at all today. She'd cried her fill of tears, enough for a lifetime, as her faithful companion had lain dying. He'd been at her side everywhere she went for so long that now she felt incomplete. Empty. A barren wasteland where her heart had once been.

She hadn't wanted to get out of bed that morning, refusing even her own duenna, Nana. Eventually her father had come and insisted that she get up, something he had not done for years. But what was the point in getting up? Her soul had not the strength to go on.

"Maria," he'd said quietly, taking a seat beside her on the bed. "I know what it is like to lose someone you love. You feel so very alone, like all is dark, and the sun will never shine again. As though all luster has gone from the world. You feel that there is no reason to ever even move again."

She had nodded at him, relieved to see that he, at least, understood. She'd stared at the simple orange tiles of her floor as he spoke, trying to resist the soothing effect of her father's voice and the comfort of his presence.

"But, and this is important, *mi querida,* not only will the night end and the sun shine, but it will do so with or without you. Fate extends her hand, and if you're not there to take it, you will miss out on a lifetime of opportunities. She will not wait for you to decide you no longer hurt."

The silence grew, and Maria had looked up at his face. The muscles on his clean-shaven jaw jumped as he worked his mouth before drawing in a ragged breath. With a steady voice, he continued. "You will always hurt. The pain will simply become easier to bear, with time."

Maria had turned away from him without saying anything, pulling her blanket back over her head. She didn't want things to get better. She wanted Alistair back.

Her father had set his hand on her shoulder and gave it a squeeze. "Remember this, if nothing else: today will happen only once. You have only today to live."

Maria had gotten out of bed after he left, more because he would have continued lecturing her about wasted time than because he'd inspired her. She'd put on a happy face and tromped about with her friends through town, teased a strange young man, and now she sewed. *Yes, Papa,* she thought, stabbing her needle through the cloth. *What a fateful day it's been.*

Her mind turned again to her dog. The moment she'd realized no amount of love and care could keep him from dying had ripped her heart from her chest. And it was her own fault. As always. She was the one who had called to him just as the wagon had come around the corner. Maria's hands slowed in their stitching and dropped into her lap.

Every time she tried to do something important, life spit in her face. Even just being born had caused her mother's death. Maria shut her eyes against the tears that threatened to push their way out. The image of her father's face from the previous night rose before her. There had been such depth of sorrow there, more than she could really comprehend. As much as she missed Alistair, and hurt from it, logic demanded she face the truth: there was worse pain awaiting her if she wasn't careful.

Blinking back her emotion, Maria picked absently at a thread on her dark skirt as she thought. She ignored the conversation that took place around her, as interesting as the honking of geese. She wanted to get out, to go somewhere, anywhere, and just be alone for a while. But to go out alone was simply not allowed.

Her father's gardens, tucked securely within the guarded walls of the *hacienda*, could provide a sense of remoteness. But the illusion of solitude didn't seem enough today. The grounds here at Casa de la Cuesta were watched as well, though not nearly as closely as her father's grounds. Normally this didn't bother her, but today it felt like being drowned by goodwill.

The sudden chiming of the grandfather clock in the hall sent a wave of relief over her as it announced her chance at freedom. Extricating herself from the gaggle of domestic geese, Maria found herself excited to get home and enjoy a quiet supper with her father. The echoes of her friends' farewells followed her out into the large hall, the ball of tension within her chest loosened with each step. As the grand, curved staircase in the entry way came into view, Maria's heart lifted. When she arrived home her father would ask her about her day, and she his, and she'd be left in peace.

The doorman opened the heavy door, and the evening sunlight slanted in, bringing with it the rich scent of roses, orchids, and coming rain. He let her out with a bow, and she thanked him with a reflexive smile that didn't reach her eyes.

As she stepped into the courtyard, she patted her leg to call Alistair to heel before catching herself. Setting her jaw, Maria lifted her head and refused to look at the empty spot between the arched pillars where he would have waited to escort her. She swept down the front steps and set out with a long stride toward home.

Before she'd left the plantation's palm-lined front drive, Maria had picked up a silent follower. The obligatory escort was just another reminder of her loss. Doña Olivia had insisted the girls always be followed, since the day Alistair had saved her life. *They'll be discreet, to give you a sense of freedom,* Maria mimicked in her mind. With Alistair at her side, she'd never needed anyone's protection. Now she felt the expanse of the unseen behind her, and the lengthening shadows made her shudder. She paused and motioned her escort-of-the-day to walk beside her.

They continued in silence in the muggy afternoon light. Maria, lost in her thoughts, retraced her steps from the night of the attack so many years ago. As before, when she reached the docks she slowed, looking out into the lake.

"You know, Señorita, it was I who was with you that night." the mestizo manservant said, breaking the silence and startling Maria. She looked at her escort for the first time and took a moment before she connected his name to his face. José. "I had been sent after you, but I was still too far away to do more than shout when I saw the man in the shadows, but the dog! It was though he knew what was coming. He'd slunk off before I even knew there was danger and leapt on the *pendejo* with the ferocity of a wild animal. He was a magnificent beast."

"That he was," Maria agreed, returning her gaze to the expansive lake.

"Though you may not have known it, that pup of yours was famous among my people."

"I am glad," she replied, a flare of pride lightening her heart for a moment.

With a sigh that released the momentary warmth in her heart, she tore her gaze from the water. Typically, the house staff did not talk to the girls, but Maria had found that, when alone, they would talk to her.

The manservant continued on. "They say that you hadn't named him until after that night. That you named him for something I said, but I've always wondered what that was."

"Alistair." Maria thought for a moment, picking at the wood of the rail before her. "It is Greek, meaning protector or guardian. I suppose, now that I think about it, that I did name him after something that was said. I'd had him for some three months and still couldn't settle on a name. When you brought me home and explained to my father, you said that Alistair was a born protector. We waited up all night for him, and when he came home, all torn up but pleased as could be with himself, I knew just what to call him."

"I don't believe I ever saw you without him, after that," José said. "I'm honored to have been a part of his naming."

Maria nodded and started again toward home. When they reached the white stucco of the *hacienda's* outer walls, she stopped him at the large, arched gate. "Thank you for your time, José. Return home safely."

"*Gracias*, Señorita. You've always been so kind." He smiled, bowed, and then disappeared into the fading evening light.

Maria watched him go. Why should he thank her for her kindness? She was just being polite, and Nana would have had a thing or two to say if she hadn't been. With a dismissive shake of her head, she stepped into the large courtyard. The gravel between the pavers crunched beneath her feet as a servant closed the heavy wooden gate behind her. A hand on her elbow made her spin, her heart in her throat.

"Pardon, I didn't mean to startle you." The British accent calmed her even before she recognized the dark-haired young man.

"Miguel," Maria said, breathless. "You gave me a fright. What are you doing here?"

"Let me escort you in, and I shall explain," Miguel said with exaggerated seriousness bowing flamboyantly. The once-fine knee-length coat he had added to his attire, just as worn as the rest of his clothing, only added to the absurdity of the movement, and Maria couldn't help but laugh. Still in his deep bow, Miguel raised his eyes to hers and winked.

For a moment, she wondered what would happen if she ignored him, but the chance for a moment of levity was too tempting. If he wanted to play a fool, then she was happy to help. Lifting her chin, Maria held up her hand. "Lead on, señor."

Miguel straightened and placed his hand under hers. They held their hands aloft as they stepped through the courtyard toward the main house. The pompous display was too much for Maria, and she broke into laughter as they reached the house. She made the mistake of looking at him as she caught her breath, and his thoroughly scandalized look sent her into another fit of laughter. Then he, too, laughed.

"Ah, I see you have met our new guest already," a booming voice said, and Maria turned toward the house. Her father, Ciro Álvarez, sat on the steps before the heavy, ornate wooden door, watching them with an amused smile. She tried to school her face, but it was hard not to smile around her father.

"Good evening, Papa." Maria moved to his side and gave him a kiss on his cheek.

"I see you've done as I suggested, *mi querida,*" Ciro said softly. "It is good to see you smile."

Maria looked at the ground, ashamed he might see she hadn't been so happy a few minutes before.

"Let me introduce you," Ciro said, his voice returning to normal as he gestured to Miguel. "Maria, meet Miguel Blanco del Mar. He's just come in on *La Solidad* and has recommended her to me as a sound ship for a shipment I need to move. Miguel, my daughter, Maria."

Maria raised her eyebrow at Miguel. He gave her a sheepish smile before dropping into a formal, and appropriate this time, bow. "A pleasure to meet you."

"The pleasure is mine." Maria curtsied and gave him a properly sweet smile, looking into his dark, green eyes.

"Excellent!" Ciro broke in. "Maria, you're just in time for supper. Come, let us eat."

Ciro led the way along the covered walkway to a patio. The area was covered and partitioned from the rest of the grounds, and the walls overflowed with flowering greenery from the gardens it overlooked. Miguel gestured for Maria to walk ahead of him. She could almost feel him behind her as they walked, and she kept her eyes resolutely on her father's back to keep from squirming.

As she stepped onto the shaded patio, Maria's eye swept over the table, taking in the four place settings. Three on one end and the last, always freshly set but never used, at the opposite end. A servant, just setting out the last of the food, bowed to them and silently retreated to the kitchen.

"I've always enjoyed being out of doors as much as possible," Ciro said as he moved to the head of the table. Maria sat in the seat beside him, motioning Miguel to the setting across from her. "And supping in the evening light when the weather cooperates is to be preferred over a stuffy dining room. Don't you think?"

"I think anything beats a ship's galley, señor," Miguel said as he sat.

Ciro laughed, slapping the table hard enough to make the plates and Maria jump. "It does indeed."

"Tell us a little about yourself, Miguel," Maria prodded, hoping that she might get better answers now that her father was present. "What brings you to Maracaibo and to my father here?"

Miguel nodded as he laid the napkin across his lap. "Well, as I told your father, I have just come in as a sailor on the merchant ship, *La Soledad.* However, my contract"—Maria thought he stressed the word strangely—"with the captain has come to an end. I've been sailing most of my life and am rather through with it, so I decided to disembark at the next port and see if the place suited me." Miguel began on his supper.

"And how does Maracaibo measure up?" Maria asked, before sipping at her drink.

"I'm still trying it out, but I like it so far." Miguel looked directly at Maria as he spoke.

She dropped her eyes to her cup, hoping he wouldn't notice the heat that rose on her cheeks.

"One of the locals directed Miguel to me. He can't remember her name, only that she was quite lovely," Ciro interjected with a twinkle in his eye, waving a bit of bread for emphasis. "In fact, Maria, Miguel here has impressed me quite a bit."

"Thank you, señor," Miguel said.

"Have you found a place to stay?" Maria asked, knowing that her friends would pester her for all the details.

"Actually, I've decided to hire him," Ciro said before Miguel could begin. "I've been thinking for some time of getting an assistant. As he'll be working very closely with me, I thought it best to have him live with us." Then, in a false whisper, he added, "It's not as though we don't have the room."

This new development left Maria speechless. A look at Miguel's startled face said it was news to him as well. Miguel recovered quickly, though, thanking Ciro. The conversation between the men moved on, and Maria withdrew into her own thoughts. The idea of Miguel living in their home, eating with them, seeing his green eyes every day filled her with feelings she'd never felt before and had no name for. They rolled over her, confusing her with their strength. She stared at her plate, listlessly pushing the food around with her fork as she fought to still the waves of emotion.

Thinking she had pushed her emotions well enough aside, she risked a glance at Miguel, who shot her a grin. Quickly looking away, she flushed again as the fluttering in her chest returned with vigor.

"Señorita?" Anita, a kitchen maid, asked quietly, nudging her shoulder. Maria looked up, startled to find they were changing the course. She hoped no one else had noticed her sudden lapse of sensibility.

"*Si*, take it." She waved Anita away. Schooling her face to look nonchalant, and with a firm grip on her emotions this time, she risked a glance back at her father and Miguel. *Miguel,* she repeated to herself, enjoying the way his name sounded in her mind, desperate to see what it felt like on her tongue. With great effort she pulled her mind back toward the conversation. To her relief, it seemed to be coming to a close.

"… won't be needing you in the morning," her father said. "I've got it managed for tomorrow."

"That'll be good. I'm in need of clothes better suited to land life, something better than tattered breeches and salt-stiff shirts. Years at sea will do a number on one's attire." He looked over at Maria. His unexpected look again startled her, and she dropped her eyes to his hands, noting how large and strong they appeared.

"Years at sea will do a number on just about everything," Ciro agreed with a chuckle. "How about you accompany Maria about the town tomorrow? She can show you to the tailor and tell you some of Maracaibo's exciting history."

Maria's eyes shot up to her father's face to find him giving her an impish smile. Thoughts raced, colliding through Maria's mind, too jumbled to form into words.

"I'd really enjoy that, Don Ciro." Miguel turned to her and raised a questioning eyebrow. "That is, if Maria doesn't mind?"

"I'd be delighted," Maria murmured, again looking at Miguel's hands. Thoughts of what those hands might feel like if she touched them invaded her mind. Unable to handle the turmoil inside any longer, Maria excused herself.

The scrape of wood against the paving stones told her that Miguel stood when she did, but she stubbornly refused to look toward him again. Keeping her eyes strictly on the door to the house, she walked with enough quiet dignity to have made Doña Olivia proud. She could feel him watching her, his gaze burning into her back as she moved. The few strides to the entrance seemed to take an eternity, and the white stucco of the arched walkway provided a tangible relief as she passed between. The moment she was out of sight of the dining patio, she fled to her room.

The safety of her room washed over her like a cool breeze as she shut the door behind her. Leaning against it, Maria inhaled deeply through her nose, attempting to calm her still- fluttering heart. But it was not willing to be calmed. *What is wrong with me?*

Maria paced the room, wringing a handkerchief in her hands, and her shoes clicking against the tiled floor. Just that morning she had thought her world was over, but now her fickle, disloyal heart would not stop obsessing over the young man downstairs. Irritation warred with wistfulness as she flung open the door to her balcony and leaned over the railing. The sweet, rich evening air rose from the gardens below, filling her lungs and worked toward stilling her mind.

Alistair was gone, and nothing could ever change that. She had loved her sweet sea-pup, and there would always be a special place for him in her heart. She took another deep breath of the fragrant air. Exhaling slowly, she felt something within her release. Just because he was gone didn't mean there wasn't anything left to be happy about.

34

A slow smile spread across her face, and she looked around sheepishly to ensure she was alone, and retreated back into her room. The bedroom stood in candlelit darkness, and not even the dim, moonlit shadows through the broad-leafed trees outside her small balcony moved. As quietly as she could manage, she whispered Miguel's name. She giggled at the silliness of her furtive behavior, yet the feel of his name on her lips was a soft caress, and the sound in her ears, sweet music. Reaching out to the vine that grew outside her balcony door, she picked a red hibiscus in full bloom. Its golden pollen dusted the air as she spun it, withdrew back into her room, and dropped onto her bed.

Maria gently stroked the large blossom, but rather than its soft petals, her thoughts lingered on the hands of a certain ex-sailor. The tanned skin certainly held within them a sure strength, and no doubt they were gentle enough to handle a kitten. Did he like kittens? She could get him one. Tied with a pretty ribbon around its neck, green to match his eyes, of course. He would take it from her, and perhaps their hands would touch for the briefest of moments …. She would look up at him through her lashes and he'd smile that beautiful smile at her. Oh, that smile.

Maria's thoughts meandered along the simple, innocent paths of the first blush of love. Eventually, she fell asleep with a smile and his name on her lips.

***

Miguel stood before the large fireplace, eyeing the bric-a-brac along the mantle, the dark wood offsetting the warm beige and subtly patterned tiles on the walls. How would it be to stay in one place long enough to accumulate such things? To have a place so entirely yours that you belonged to it as much as it belonged to you? A pain sliced through his heart as the image of his father's cabin rose before his eyes. Irritated, he slammed the memory and the pain aside. That place would never be his; he'd left it behind three ships ago.

"What do you think of it, young Miguel?" Don Ciro's voice boomed behind him, and Miguel spun, his hand automatically reaching for the knife at his hip.

"It speaks to me of stability," he said, irritated at himself for being so lost in his thoughts that he hadn't heard his employer enter. Don Ciro smiled at him, and for a moment Miguel was taken aback at how genuine it seemed.

"And what do you think of my daughter?"

Well, that certainly wasn't the direction he'd thought this would take. Miguel dropped his hand from the knife and thought a moment, trying to decide how to not insult this kind but powerful man. He certainly wouldn't want to hear how his daughter had watched Miguel during dinner, or the way her face had flushed whenever Miguel met her dark eyes. This would certainly complicate things.

"She's young," he said, settling on the truth. "And rather taken with me, I think. Please tell me she has a beau."

36

Don Ciro laughed and sat before the fireplace, gesturing for Miguel to do likewise. He sat in the chair opposite his employer, sinking down into the overly soft cushion.

"She's sixteen," Don Ciro said as Miguel dragged himself forward to sit on the edge of a chair that wanted to suck him into its depths. "And she's recently gone through some heartbreak. I'm sure it's nothing serious. I'm just glad to see her smile again."

Miguel nodded. He hoped so too. He was not interested in entanglements, just stable employment.

"She's also headstrong and smart, when she wants to be, but in many ways she is still very young. Maria knows nothing of danger or the forces that move this world outside the protection of these walls." Don Ciro leaned forward, and Miguel found himself mirroring the action. "I intend for it to stay that way."

Miguel nodded again. If he'd wanted a dull life, this had been the wrong place to come. The pistol that rested, loaded but uncocked in his jacket, pressed against his ribs. No, a dull life was definitely not something he was interested in. "What do I need to know?"

Chapter 3

MARIA WOKE bursting with joy. It was going to be a beautiful, wonderful day, she was sure of it. The morning sun glinted off the colored tiles of her floor, casting playful shapes across the walls and ceiling. The birds sang as they flirted with the hibiscus at her window, and the flowers cast their sweet floral scents into the air. Maria hopped out of bed and whistled for Alistair. Then, without waiting for him, she pulled on her robe and threw open the door–and stopped dead.

The world crashed down around her like a shattered stained-glass window. The joy that had filled her the moment before turned to ash in her mouth as she turned back to the empty rug near the foot of her bed. There was no Alistair anymore. The bright morning sun glared harsh and profane; the birdsong now a callous mock of her reality. The familiar lump rose in her throat as she stepped back into her room and shut the door. Sliding down the door frame, she hugged her knees to her chest as the tears flowed down her cheeks.

The sobbing lasted only a few minutes before the emptiness in her chest left her eyes dry. A soft rap on the door made her hastily wipe her still damp cheeks. She didn't want her father to know she'd been crying again.

"Señorita?" her nursemaid called softly. "Let me in, *querida*. It is time to be up. You have appointments today."

Grudgingly, Maria moved to the side just enough to let the door open. "The world is a dark and dreary place for me today. Surely everyone else living in the sun can find their way without me for one day," Maria muttered as she stood before Nana could get after her for sitting on the floor.

"Dramatic today, aren't we?" Nana walked directly to the closet, and pulled out two dresses. "Come now, you mustn't wander around in just your robe anymore. You're practically a woman grown. With a guest in the house, it simply wouldn't be proper."

"Guest?" Maria raised a skeptical eyebrow and gestured to the dress closest to her, a pale green one with tan embroidery. She wished she had grey, to match her mood.

"Forgotten already?" Nana tsked. "A young thing like you shouldn't have the memory of an old woman like me."

"Your memory is fine, Nana. More than fine. You could probably tell my father more about himself than he could." Despite the empty ache in her chest, the familiar banter lifted her spirits a little.

"Pshaw! I'm older than you can imagine, silly girl. The stories I could tell ...." The nursemaid helped Maria with the dress.

"What, you mean like the two evil ancients of the Wayuu? Or of Si'a stealing jewels for the Earth goddess?" Maria threaded her corset while Nana tied the skirt.

"It was for Pulowi of the sea, not the earth, *chica,* as you well know."

"And what would poor Doña Olivia say if she knew I had grown up on such heathen tales of the natives?" Maria said with mock severity, pulling her laces tight. "Or that you've been trying to sneak Wayuunaiki words into my brain since before I could walk?"

"I don't find that woman's opinion of what I do with my charges to be worth a goat's rear end, and you know it." Nana helped Maria with her jacket.

"What of my mother, then, what would she think of it?" Maria rolled her shoulders in her jacket, helping it settle properly.

"I helped raise your mother, same as I helped raise you, silly girl. She wouldn't mind any more than you do." Nana stood back, inspecting her.

Maria reached out, taking Nana's hand and pulling her close. "Tell me more about her; you knew her better than anyone. What was she like? What was her favorite thing to do as a child?"

"Bah," Nana said, shaking herself loose from Maria and steering her toward the dresser. "You know as well as I do your father—"

"My father refuses to talk about her." Maria picked up her brush and savagely brushed her hair. Once her father's wishes were brought up, she knew she'd lost. "That's no reason for you not to."

Nana took the brush from her and gently worked through the long, black locks. "Your father didn't want to share her with others, and while I may not agree entirely with his motives, I will respect his wishes in this."

Maria mouthed along with the familiar phrase, and made a face at Nana. The old woman gave her a sly smile in the mirror

"Your hair is very fine. It reminds me of hers."

Maria clutched at the tidbit of information. It was a small success, but a success nonetheless. Any information about her mysterious mother was to be cherished. Nana changed the subject, and they continued to banter as they worked on Maria's hair. By the time they were done, Maria found herself with a small but genuine smile, though her heart remained weighed down.

"I think Miguel's been waiting on you for breakfast," the old duenna whispered with a conspiratorial wink as Maria stood to leave.

A momentary surge of happiness rushed through Maria's chest, but, unwilling to be subdued, the hurt from her lost friend fought against it, plunging her back into her melancholy. "How kind of him," she responded.

Nana sighed as Maria went out the door.

Maria focused on the soft rustle of her skirt moving around her legs as she walked, her eyes morosely on the floor before her as she descended the stairs. The feelings that she had around Miguel confused and angered her. She was in mourning for Alistair, and it just wasn't *right* that anything, especially this boy, should show up out of the blue and invade her life and her home, and—

"Oof!" Maria's thoughts were interrupted abruptly as she ran into something that shouldn't have been in the middle of the stairs.

"*Buenos días,* Señorita." Miguel smiled as he steadied her.

"*Disculpe*; I didn't see you." Maria's heart raced as much from the shock of having run into him as from the physical contact. Heat rose in her cheeks as she took the hand he offered. Though his skin had a roughness about it, his grip contained a sure and gentle strength. She held back a giggle at the fluttering in her stomach as she realized how accurate her estimation of his hands had been the night before. "*Buenos días,* Miguel. Have you eaten yet this morning?"

"A healthy appetite is something to be appreciated in a woman." He flashed a smile that dazzled her. Unwilling to get caught gazing into his gorgeous green eyes, she looked away, noting that he wore the clothes from the night before. "No, Maria," he said, that smile still in his voice. "I have not yet eaten. Would you care to breakfast with me?"

"It would be my pleasure," Maria responded automatically. Rather than letting her hand go as she'd expected, Miguel set it into the crook of his elbow, and her heart took flight, finally breaking free of the mire that had held it down. The heat of his body surprised her, bleeding through his rough-spun shirt and into her hand as he led her out the front door, and along the loggia of the main house. She slipped her hand from his arm when they reached the dining patio, ardently hoping he hadn't felt her reaction.

They sat across from each other at the outdoor table, a bowl of fruit, colorful and fragrant, sitting between them. The silence moved from comfortable to awkward as neither she nor Miguel reached toward the food.

Well Doña Olivia, how would you get out of this one, eh? Maria fiddled with her napkin in her lap, staring at her plate, at the fruit, at anything but him.

After what seemed like an eternity Miguel cleared his throat. "Well," he said, "it looks like it is going to be a nice day for a tour around the town, don't you think?"

"I suppose it is for now," she said, utterly relieved. Leave it to the British to talk about the weather. She smiled at him. "Though it will, without a doubt, become annoyingly warm and wet this afternoon."

Miguel suppressed a smile and handed her a mango. "We'll just have to find ourselves a cool, dry place by then. Do you know of any place suitable?"

Maria laughed as she took the fruit and cut it open. "I doubt there is such a place in all of Maracaibo this time of year."

"What, then, do you typically do when it gets unbearably warm and wet?" Miguel took a yellow passion fruit, and Maria raised her eyebrow at his use of a belt knife rather than the provided cutlery. He met her eyes, raised his own eyebrow, and popped the fruit into his mouth. Maria rolled her eyes at his silliness and stood.

"Come; I'll show you," Maria said, waving the mango at him to follow.

Miguel grabbed a mango of his own as he stood and followed her through the garden. The covered walkway between the buildings artfully overflowed with foliage on either side, it's arching pillars framing the garden before him. Near the corner of the main house, the long leaves of a roble cast strategic shadows across it all.

"You know," Miguel began as he stepped up beside her, "it's been such a long time since I've been in a real garden, surrounded by so many lovely plants and things."

"Why no, I didn't know, but I appreciate you enlightening me." Maria gave him a playful shove.

"I'm offended!" Miguel set his nose pompously into the air.

44

"Well, you should be!" Maria waved her half-eaten mango under his nose with her other hand set firmly on her hip. He burst out laughing, taking the mango from her. It warmed her to have made him smile.

"Well, I never!" Maria gave him a thoroughly scandalized look and walked away with her head held high.

Still laughing, Miguel caught up with her in two long strides and again set her hand in his elbow. Maria grinned as she steered him toward the courtyard.

"In all seriousness, I do love a well-kept garden. Especially ones that are so full that you can almost feel the wilderness just waiting for a chance to push through," Miguel said wistfully, pulling a large, ball-shaped pink blossom from the tree that stood before the *hacienda's* gates. "I find them full of such beauty, I think that's one of the reasons I chose to stop here. There's just something incredibly alluring about the jungles. More so here than any I've seen before."

Maria nodded as they passed through the smaller side gate. "I know what you mean. I find the jungle sounds comforting. On clear nights, you can hear it here in the *hacienda*, as though it's come right up to the walls. I've never actually been all the way out to the jungle, and just thinking about it fills me with nervousness. And yet, there's a longing, too. I even dream about it sometimes."

"That's pretty brave of you, I think." Miguel popped the last of the mango into his mouth before continuing. "Not the dreaming, I mean. I doubt there are many women who would willingly brave a jungle, especially with all the wild animals and the natives."

"I'm not so worried about the natives. There's been peace between us and them for some dozen years now. Mestizos work in the city and the plantations. My father employs several, and they've never given me any bother."

"I'm glad to hear it." Miguel guided her to the side of the road to let a wagon pass. "Tell me more about Maracaibo. What is interesting about it?"

Maria laughed. "What do you want to know?"

"Just anything. How old is it?"

"That's an interesting question, actually," Maria said with a smug smile, secretly proud of the stubbornness of her people. "The city itself has actually been built three times. The first time was in 1529 by Ambrossius Ehinger, an Hessian, after conquering the Coquivoca, who were native to the area. He named the city *Neu-Nürnberg* and the lake after their chief, Mara, who was killed in the fighting. The Spanish renamed the city Maracaibo when we took possession of it, and that name has stuck. They abandoned the city a few years later. It has been reestablished twice more since then."

"The Gulf of Venezuela is heavily sailed by pirates," Miguel said. "Is there much history of raids here?"

Maria nodded, noting that he was still wearing his cutlass. Had he slept with the thing strapped to his hip? "Some. Not as much recently, but in the early 1600s

46

there were a lot more. The most famous, of course, being when Henry Morgan attacked the city about seventy years ago. He moved on to Gibraltar, which is farther into the lake. They tried to block his escape back out to the Caribbean, but after he destroyed two of the ships blocking his way, the third surrendered."

"What about the natives? Do they fight with the Spanish much or is there peace?"

"Well, like I said, there's been a sort of peace for about a dozen years. The Wayuu to the north have organized a couple of major rebellions, the first at the turn of the century, and then again when I was four years old. I can't imagine there should be more strife from them."

Miguel nodded and changed the topic, asking about her favorite memories. She told him of the various adventures she and her friends had had with her dog. Excited to share, Maria led them through the business district to the dock where she'd first seen Alistair.

"I can still remember the crazy accent the man used!" Maria screwed up her face as she switched to English. "'This li'l fella needs a home,' he said. 'A ship hardly be a place for a lil' thing to grow up. Take care of 'im, and he'll be as good to you as 'is mother's been to me.'" Maria grinned wryly as Miguel laughed at her attempted accent.

"That's about the worst slaughtering of English I've ever heard! I've known some sailors with atrocious accents, but never with a Spanish lilt to their cockney."

"Well, see if I ever share anything with you again," Maria said with a smile.

"But I don't think I've ever heard my native tongue so sweetly abused." He gave her a wink that made her blush. "You'll have to do it again for me sometime."

Maria laughed and rolled her eyes. She'd never known a man to be so silly and inclined to laugh. Her father laughed, but he was never silly. Most of the young men the Doña allowed them to socialize with were stuffy and wrapped up in their own interests, or too shy to speak coherently.

They continued on, and she pointed out the stand in the market where they'd once stolen some fruit. Elisa, Betania, and Selena, of course, had gotten little more than a lecture from Doña Olivia. Maria's father, however, had repaid the merchant twice the value of the stolen fruit and then made her work off the debt with him.

"I'm sure it would have been worse if my father hadn't intervened," Maria said. "But I wasn't worried; Papa is always able to make things right."

"You really love your father, don't you?" Miguel stopped near the berth of *La Soledad.*

"Of course." A smile grew on Maria's face. How could she possibly express to him all that made up her father? "He is a giant among men, good and kind and patient. He can do almost anything he puts his mind to." *Almost.* The thought put a crack in her smile, and she shook her head.

"You're fortunate to have him, then."

"What about your father?" Maria asked.

Miguel shrugged. "He died a few years ago."

Maria wasn't sure what to say to that.

Miguel started up the gangplank, but stopped, turning back to her. "Maria, you do know …."

She raised her eyebrow at his hesitation. "I know a lot of things."

Emotions flitted across his face, and she wondered if what he settled on saying would be what he meant to say. Finally he shook his head, and gave her a wink. "You know, you should stay ashore while I go get my pay. I'll be right back."

"I'll be here." Maria rolled her eyes at him and leaned back against a stanchion. So, no, he hadn't said what he'd meant to. Probably something about missing her father if he died, as if that was something that might happen. Not likely. Don Ciro was in his prime, and he would be around to see his grandchildren get married and to guide and help her whenever she needed him.

When Miguel returned, they continued their tour, talking and enjoying each other's company as the day wore on.

"Maria," Miguel cut in when they stopped at the market for a bite to eat. "The food is as lovely as the company, but eventually, I will need to stop at the tailor's to be fitted for some new clothes."

Heat crept up Maria's neck. How could she have forgotten? "Of course. This way." They ate in a comfortable silence as they walked along the colorful, noisy streets to the tailor's.

"Do you think the musicians plan their performances?" Miguel asked as they turned down a street and the ambient music changed smoothly from one cadence to another, more somber one.

Maria laughed. "I'd never actually noticed before. I suppose there is always music here, isn't there? I think I'd go crazy if I lived in town; there'd be no peace from it."

"I like it. It's like the heartbeat of the place."

They slowed, and Maria gestured to the tailor's shop. "Miguel?"

He turned toward her with a half-smile, waiting for her to continue.

"Why did you use the names Elisa and I suggested?"

Miguel hesitated only a moment. "I thought they sounded nice."

"But what is wrong with your real name?"

"Miguel is my real name. Well, Michael is my real name, but I thought I'd go with the more Hispanic sound. It's easier to say." Despite his nonchalant tone, he had tensed at the question, not unlike her father did when asked about her mother. Perhaps she'd be able to get it out of him later.

"*Bienvenido!*" A voice called from within the shop, and Miguel and Maria turned to see a short, pudgy man waddle out to meet them. A smile lit his face when he recognized her.

"What can I make for you, señor?" the tailor asked Miguel, gesturing them into the shop.

"Clothes, I imagine," Miguel said with a wink for Maria.

"Miguel has hired on as my father's assistant," Maria cut in before the tailor could respond. "His extended time at sea has left him somewhat bereft of suitable attire, and Don Álvarez requests he be properly outfitted."

"Of course, señorita. As you say." The tailor gave her a slight bow and turned his hawk-eyed gaze on Miguel.

He stood a little straighter as the tailor accosted him with his measuring tape. Maria turned to go but turned back at a strangled sound from Miguel.

"Don't abandon me," Miguel mouthed to her over the short man's shoulder.

Maria laughed. "I'll be down the street at the general store. Come find me when you're done."

"If I can remember where it is," Miguel called after her as she stepped through the door.

Chapter 4

T HE HEAT AND humidity neared the point of insufferability when Miguel found Maria perusing through the market. She stood in the shade of her parasol, in her pale green dress accentuating her gentle curves, and her glossy black hair tumbling down her back. One hand held the parasol lazily against her shoulder, spinning it absently to cast dancing patterns of light across her skirts. The other held a book up for inspection. Some of the gloom she'd worn about her like a cloak the first time he'd seen her had reappeared. It wasn't right; she was meant to laugh.

Miguel stepped up behind her and leaned over her shoulder to set his face beside hers. "This is not the general store."

Maria gasped and spun, moving to hit his intruding face with the book, which he prevented with a deft block. "You …!"

"Me." Miguel took the book from her hand and looked at it. *Robinson Crusoe*. "This is a good book. Not only does it contain an entertaining story, but I hear it's good for hitting people in the face."

"So you've read it before?"

"No, but I have nearly been hit in the face with it before, and I hold the wielder of such a weapon in the highest regard as an authority on things with which to hit me in the face."

"If you're not going to purchase that, please put it down," the skinny merchant running the booth said, wringing his hands.

Miguel turned to Maria, offering her the book.

"Have you really read it?" Maria asked. "Is it any good?"

"A man shipwrecked on a jungle island? You would like it."

She hesitated a moment longer before taking it from him, and the merchant visibly relaxed. How would it be to not be treated like an untrustworthy barnacle? Well, he'd had a taste of that when he'd met with Señor Álvarez, and he'd liked it. Perhaps with time, people would stop looking at him askance. He gave a wry grin as Maria finished her transaction with the merchant, telling him to charge her father and have the book delivered. Well, time and a better accent.

Miguel tucked her free hand into the crook of his arm as they moved on. He enjoyed the gentle weight of her hand on his arm, like an anchor keeping him from wandering adrift in the world. A cool breeze gave a sharp contrast to the heavy heat that had been growing since the morning, cooling the sweat that gathered on his neck.

"Maria, it appears to be getting a bit warm and damp." Miguel dabbed at the sweat on his forehead and neck with a kerchief.

"Miguel," Maria replied. "That is an understatement."

Miguel discreetly watched the color rising in her cheeks, the blush enlivening the smooth, olive-toned skin. "Maria, I seem to recall you mentioning that you have a remedy for the heat and forthcoming rain." He hoped she would glance up at him with those large, dark eyes.

"Miguel, I certainly did." She gave him a coy smile, and he wished for another cool breeze to save him from the growing heat.

"Would you, could you tell me how you stand it?" *Careful there, Mick.* The inner voice of warning nudged at him.

"I would, I could … but I shan't." Maria gave him a sweet smile, and he pushed aside his concerns. Being friendly wouldn't cause any harm, and she needed distraction from her gloom.

"Fair maiden, you are cruel!" Miguel grabbed at his heart, and her laughter filled him.

She was so easy to talk to, and so quick to smile. A welcome change from the dour, stifling moods of his shipmates. It felt so good to make someone smile again. She was like fresh air blowing in through a stale hold, bringing with it all the promises of a new day. Of a new life.

"Ah, I recognize this place," Miguel said as they passed the crossroads where she had left him the day before.

"What powers of recollection you have."

"Indeed. It is where, yesterday, four angels left me, taking with them the light of the world. We now follow their course."

"I see. Angels, you say? I've never seen any angels around here." Maria elbowed him playfully as they walked. "Perhaps you can tell me about them?"

"Well, I recall they were about your age. Two were sisters, one their cousin, and one who just didn't quite fit in at all. Perhaps you could tell me more."

"I suppose I ought to prepare you. I wouldn't want you to inadvertently insult one."

"They might smite me, and then where would I be?" Back on *La Soledad*? Never. He kicked a stone, more viciously than he meant to, off to the side of the road. Every step seemed to plant him more firmly ashore, which was fine by him.

"The youngest, Elisa, and the oldest, Betania, are sisters, Señoritas de la Cuesta. Doña Olivia Palomo and Don Sergio Díaz are their parents, Señor and Señora de la Cuesta." The girls' family were plantation owners, then. It didn't surprise him. They wore their wealth and privilege in their walk, in the way they held their heads, in the way they looked at him as he came ashore, and they didn't even know it.

Maria had paused, and he nodded to her to continue. "Selena is Elisa's cousin. Doña Olivia took her in when her mother, Doña Olivia's sister, Natalia, died."

"So Elisa and Betania are sisters, and Selena is their cousin. That explains them, but how do you fit in?" Miguel asked.

"I thought you just said I didn't," Maria poked him in the arm. "My father knew Señor Díaz from when he was with the East India Trading Company." Miguel cringed at the mention of the Company. Don Ciro hadn't mentioned that. "So when my father settled here, they became business partners, and Doña Olivia helped to raise me."

"But what about your mother?"

"There's not much to tell." Maria shrugged, shifting the parasol on her shoulder. He wondered how much it actually helped with the heat. "My parents married before my father settled here. She died shortly after I was born. Nana told me that he was so heartbroken over it all that he couldn't bear staying near her family anymore, so we came to Maracaibo. Nobody here knew her other than Nana and Papa, and so no one really talks about her."

"Not even your father?"

"He doesn't like to talk about her. I think …." Maria smiled sadly and gave his arm a slight squeeze, as though trying to pull something lost back to herself. "I think it hurts too much. I asked him once, when I was very young. He got upset and locked himself in his study. I didn't see him again for three days."

Maria turned him down a palm-lined drive that, from the description Don Ciro had given him the night before, Miguel assumed led to the Díaz plantation. A rich earthy aroma rose around them as they neared the large house. The building surrounded an elegant courtyard on three sides, with a fountain in the middle. Arcades lined the building in a similar fashion to the *hacienda*, but with none of the Álvarez home's warmth. The two story building had a stark elegance, from its patterned drive to its ornate decor.

"Casa de la Cuesta, I take it?" Miguel asked.

Maria nodded as she removed her hand from Miguel's arm. "It overlooks both the plantation grounds and much of Maracaibo itself. From the topmost stories, you can even see Lake Maracaibo."

The heavy wood door opened with an unsettling silence as the elderly butler let them in, instructing them to wait in the foyer while he sent for Doña Olivia. The enormous room felt cavernous to Miguel, with its musty, humid air, cold stone flooring, and extravagant tiling. Arrogant bits of art were scattered here and there. It probably made some statement about their lineage or some such thing. A person could get lost in a place like this, and not just physically. Maria stood apart from him, and the loss of her steadying hand only intensified the feeling.

The crisp click of a woman's footsteps drew Miguel's gaze. The woman gave an appearance of height that she didn't actually have. With her upswept dark blond hair and eyes that managed to look down at him despite her lesser height; she could only be the lady of the house.

With a formal air that ill-suited her, Maria stepped forward to introduce them. "Doña Olivia, may I present Miguel Blanco del Mar, newly arrived in Maracaibo on the merchant ship *La Soledad* and is currently employed by my father."

Miguel bowed.

"Miguel, may I present Doña Olivia Palomo Mingo, Señora de la Cuesta."

"*Mucho gusto,* Miguel." Doña Olivia inclined her head. "It is a pleasure to finally meet you. My daughters have said much about you."

"*Mucho gusto,* Doña Olivia." This woman was about as friendly as an iceberg. Well, never let it be said he didn't try to be friendly. Miguel gave her a playful smile. "I hope it's only good things they've been saying."

Doña Olivia actually smiled. Imagine that. "Here come my daughters. Miguel, my daughters, Betania and Elisa Díaz Palomo, Señoritas de la Cuesta."

The young women in question rushed down the sweeping, curved staircase until a sharp look from Doña Olivia slowed them. Elisa and Betania curtsied beside their mother. Sweet Betania kept her eyes down, but Elisa, with her eyes full of fire and trouble, looked him full in the face.

The Doña gestured to her other side where the fourth angel appeared from the hallway, dark like her aunt but taller than her cousins. "And my niece and ward, Selena Abano Palomo." Selena's curtsey, as perfectly proper as the others', spoke only of mild curiosity.

"Betania, Elisa, Selena, this is Miguel Blanco del Mar—" Doña Olivia arched her eyebrow at Elisa, who had snickered at his surname "—whom you have already met."

Miguel bowed again, clutching his hands into fists to avoid doing something outrageous, just to see what would happen. *Don't be an idiot.*

Selena gave a nod to Maria and in a soft voice said, "Why, Maria, dear, it would seem you've picked up another sea pup."

Doña Olivia gave her a sharp, reproving look. Now what was that about?

"Only this time she wasted no time naming him!" Elisa added. Were they actually comparing him to the dog? The señoritas all giggled at the quip, and even Doña Olivia hid a grin. It stung, but he hid it behind a bewildered look at Maria. She blushed and looked away. So the comparison was to the dog. But Maria hadn't laughed. He clung to that.

"That's enough," Doña Olivia commanded, still trying to hide her amusement. "All of you will go, now!"

The four girls curtsied again and practically scampered off.

"Not you, please," Doña Olivia said to Miguel. "I'd like a word with you. If you will follow me?"

"Certainly, Señora," Miguel again bowed, all playfulness gone, and followed the mistress of the house.

***

"Did you *see* the look on his face?" Selena laughed when they reached the girls' private garden.

"Honestly, what kind of surname is Blanco del Mar?" Elisa chimed in, careful to stay beneath the awning despite the fact that the rain had not yet begun.

"*His* face? Did you see your mother's face?" Maria shot back.

"If I got to choose my surname, it would be something far more romantic." Elisa removed her shoes to play in the sheltered pond beneath a canopy of well-manicured trees, their branches brilliant with their yellow and pink blooms.

"That really wasn't a nice thing to say, you know." Betania took a seat near the edge of the pond.

"You should lighten up, learn to have a little fun." Selena splashed water at Betania, who shrieked.

"Did you know that the British take their husband's surname when they get married?" Elisa went on.

"What were you doing with him, Maria?" Betania moved to a spot further from the water, trying to maintain the dignity of being the oldest.

"Yes, tell us!" Selena insisted.

"I don't know that I would want to change my name. Elisa Blanco del Mar. It just sounds so ...." Elisa shrugged and tossed a flower petal into the water.

"Bland," Betania finished for her sister, and Elisa nodded.

"Well, turns out my father invited him to stay with us for a time," Maria said, determined not to blush. She could imagine how they'd turn on her like hounds at the first scent of her wild emotions.

"What?!" Elisa, finally shocked out of her own thoughts, looked up. "You mean you really have taken in another sea dog?"

"He's not a dog," Selena said.

"But a more handsome sea dog I've never seen." Elisa smiled. "Tell us what he's like?"

"Did you have supper with him?" Betania asked.

"Did you take him home with you last night?" Selena asked.

"Were you alone together?" Betania asked.

"Yes, we had supper together, but no, we weren't alone; my father was there." Maria tried to answer the questions as quickly as they came. "He had already spoken to my father and was there when I got home."

As Maria paused for breath, more comments flooded in to fill the space.

"I wonder if we could get him to stay with us."

"He's so handsome! Did he say why he wears that cutlass?"

"Does he talk a lot? He looked so serious today."

"Do you think he's seen many battles?"

"Don't you think his eyes are so dreamy?"

Maria gave up on following what everyone was saying and sat down on the edge of the fountain with a flower in her hand, trailing it along in the water.

"My goodness!" Doña Olivia's voice rang out over them, "You'd think none of you had ever seen a young man before."

Maria jerked up her head, looking in Doña Olivia's direction and hoping Miguel had not heard them. Relief and disappointment flooded through her to realize that he was not there. She wrinkled her nose at the sensation.

"Where's Miguel, Mama?" Elisa asked.

"He remembered some errands Don Álvarez requested that he do today. He will return later to escort Maria home." At the crestfallen looks of her charges Doña Olivia added, "Don't get too attached to him. There are plenty of other men in Maracaibo. Plenty who are not sailors."

Selena turned away at the last, and Maria wondered if Doña Olivia saw how much her words hurt. The older woman left the girls to themselves, and Maria wished she had just brought the book with her, rather than sending it home.

Maria moved to the bench beside Betania and leaned back, resting against the large, sturdy trunk that stood beside it, its long thin leaves reaching out far above them. She closed her eyes and just listened. It had been a long day so far, and her feet ached. If it weren't for the risk that Elisa would start asking her questions again, Maria would have removed her shoes and rested her feet in the cool pond. The babble of the water that ran into their little pond mixed with the tentative return of birdsong as the girls settled to their interests.

She inhaled, savoring the full feel of the air that smelt of forthcoming rain, but not yet. There was a telltale change in the air, in the sound of the wind, in the very trees it seemed, that stole over the world just before the rain would fall. And it was not yet.

A rustle of paper beside her caused her to open her eyes, and Maria sat up. Betania startled, and quickly folded up the letter she'd been reading, setting her hand over it.

"What's that?" Maria asked with a grin, reaching for the letter.

"Nothing." Betania jerked it away and shoved it into her pocket.

"Really? It looked like a letter to me."

"It's just a letter from Rosalina," Betania mumbled.

Maria grinned. "And full of her brother's regards, no doubt."

Betania blushed, and Maria nudged her gently. "Don't worry. I won't tell anyone you've got secret designs on a certain darkly handsome young man."

"You're one to speak of handsome young men," Betania retorted.

Maria's heart stopped. Did she know? How could she know? Frantically, Maria ran through her behavior from the last day. Certain she hadn't done anything out of the ordinary, her heart resumed its normal beat. "I don't know what you mean."

Betania's light laughter sounded right at home along with the garden's birdsong. "I'm not blind. You light up when he's around. I thought you'd be under a little storm cloud for at least a month when you lost Alistair, but you showed up today actually smiling."

Maria shook her head. "It's not like that. He's a silly fool, and he makes me laugh, that's all. Besides, it's like your mother says. He's a sailor. He'll leave eventually, and I want a stable life with my husband at home with me. And a sailor could never give me that." But even as the words left her mouth, Maria felt a twinge of shame. Her father had been a sailor once, and he was a fine man. The best, really.

"But what if it's love?" Betania said. The wistfulness in her voice made Maria suspect she wasn't thinking of Maria's feelings.

"I wouldn't know." What did she know of love? The image of her father's pained face when he thought of her mother came to mind. Nana said he'd loved her mother very much. "But I imagine real love takes more than a day."

***

Miguel walked around the cocoa plantation, the hot, heavy breeze moving around him, full and earthy smelling. So unlike the briny, cold air of life on the ocean, always overlaid with the aromas of wood and tar and sweat. Walking beside a long, thick row of shoulder-high cacao trees to one side and a row of tall, shady palm trees on the other—a pattern repeated across the entire field—brought fuzzy memories of running along the neat rows of another field. Memories buried by years and half a world's worth of water, and without a need for revival.

Don Ciro's proposal intrigued him, but he was more excited at the prospect of stable, respectable work. Not that sailing hadn't been respectable; it just hadn't been the same the last few years. He wanted more from his life than endless repetition of menial tasks, strict orders, and constant discipline. He believed now, after talking with Doña Olivia, that this job would certainly fit that bill.

"So, Don Ciro has taken you on to be his 'assistant,' has he?" Doña Olivia had said as she led him toward a parlor, in the opposite direction from the girls.

"Yes, Señora."

"He's been considering doing just that for a long time but never found the right man. I'm sure he has already explained to you what he will be holding you responsible for, *si*?"

"Indeed, Doña Olivia. Don Álvarez is a very thorough employer." Miguel gave her a level look. Despite his earlier misgivings, the woman was treating him with respect. A welcome surprise.

"That he is, Miguel. That he is." Doña Olivia strode toward the door and gazed over the gardens with their wide gravel paths, almost maze-like hedges, and flowers of all colors accentuating it all. Miguel followed, humbled by the shadow of respectability Don Ciro had cast over him. He would work hard to avoid disappointing such a man.

"It would appear that Maria trusts you," Doña Olivia continued. "She's a nice girl, but naïve. Ciro Álvarez is a good man but not one to cross. You mustn't ever be less than serious about what he's hired you to do, do you understand that?"

Miguel did, and he'd told her so. He was never less than serious about paid work. Satisfied with his reply, she had instructed him to familiarize himself with the plantation grounds. Before they'd parted, she'd added a warning.

"These girls are not to be hurt." Her voice had all the grave authority of a captain, and he'd stood straighter, despite himself. "Don't get too close to them. If I ever find that you broke their hearts, you will wish you'd never been born."

Miguel's hand had twitched toward a salute, and he'd gripped his cutlass instead, bowing with a "Yes, mum."

Doña Olivia had given him a curt nod, then swooped away the way she'd come.

Miguel rested his hand on his cutlass as he explored, reaching the end of the row. As he turned back toward the gardens and the house, the warm rain finally began. It felt so right to have the weapon there again, like an old friend at his side. The only true friend he'd ever had.

He hadn't lied when he'd told Maria that he was tired of a sailor's life, but this had been just another port, a stopping-off point on the way to something better. He could hear the girls' laughter coming from beyond the walls of their enclosed garden. He walked along the wall, looking for flaws and footholds, anything that would help him watch over it and its patrons. One laugh stood out to him over the rest, musical and entrancing. Perhaps Maracaibo could become home.

Chapter 5

T HE WORST OF the heat had passed with the afternoon sun, and the rain had become a light misting in the air. A fresh carpeting of yellow tree blossoms covered much of the garden. Maria yawned and stretched, flipping through the pages of the book she'd been reading.

"I couldn't agree more." Betania closed her own book.

"Shall we attempt to find our lost puppy?" Elisa asked, tossing a flower into the pond. "I hope he hasn't wandered too far, or that Mama didn't scare him off."

"I'm sure he has plenty of more important things to do for my father than wait around for us." Maria waited for her friends to pass through the gate before following.

"Why, Miguel, wherever have you been?" Selena called out from beyond the gate, her voice dripping with honey.

Surely she was making fun?

"Ah, lovely señorita, I have but been in search of thee all day." Miguel's playful tenor voice and British accent were unmistakable, and a bubble of joy fizzled through Maria as she followed her friends out the gate.

"Just me?" Selena asked, and Maria hid a smile at the sight of his flamboyant bow.

"Alas, no. Thee and thy companions three," he said with mock seriousness. He bowed to each of them as they giggled. "I'm afraid I have been terribly lost."

"It is most fortuitous, then, that we have found you." Elisa stepped up to him and took his arm.

Miguel's gaze paused on Maria for a moment and then turned back to Elisa as she led him down the path. Or was Maria just imagining things? Selena took up Maria's arm, jolting her from her thoughts. Shrugging, Maria linked her arm through Betania's and the five of them returned to the house.

***

Maria thought Miguel enjoyed himself as the girls led him on a tour of the de la Cuesta plantation. After an early supper, Miguel suggested that he and Maria be on their way, and she was only too happy for the excuse to leave.

"I'm still not convinced that going through the town is truly the fastest way," Miguel said as they walked through the bustle along the docks. A parrot swooped down across the street, making Miguel duck and push Maria behind him. She laughed and pushed back as the bird continued into the trees that stood between the nearest warehouse. He gave it a rueful look and straightened his jacket. "If I had to guess, I'd say you just love looking at the lake."

"Then you'd guess wrong." Maria slowed, leaning against a post to look out over the water. The waves moved serenely, lapping against the hulls of the many ships that waited in the harbor. "As much as I love the lake, it *is* actually the fastest way to get to the eastern side of town by foot."

An awareness of how close Miguel stood to her as he watched the people on the dock distracted her from her thoughts. He shifted, drawing her eye as he checked his cutlass and leaned his other hand casually atop the pistol she had seen just beneath his coat. The restless murmur of the people mixed with the harbor's water, filling the silence between them, spiced by the familiar scents of lake water, life, and food. The *palafitos* floated in their distant silence atop it all as the shadows stretched across the lake.

"Do you suppose life is any simpler there?"

"What do you mean?" Miguel tilted his head toward her.

"I mean—do you think the Marabinos have it easier? It looks so simple and peaceful, living your life out on a lake. No need to wear a certain dress to dinner or hold to useless formalities. No loss, no pain, just floating on the lake. Is life simpler on the water?" Maria kept her eyes forward.

Miguel turned, looking for a moment at the floating village. "No, I don't believe that it is. I've been many places in this world, seen many types of people, and they all have their formalities. Their own cultures." Miguel turned back toward the market and Maria watched him from the corner of her eye. "Loss and pain? That seems to be inherent in human nature. On the sea, death becomes an intricate part of life, like work. It is simply what life is."

Maria looked south, across the narrow neck of water toward the open lake. Somehow, that didn't seem right. Surely there was some place a person could just be happy? "My father told me that when a person dies at sea, they're sewn into a canvas bag and given to the water. He says that most sailors think it's bad luck to have a dead body on board."

"Indeed."

He watched her turn back to the water as the nightly Catatumbo storm gathered in the distance. Miguel's shipmates had told him of it, but this was his first chance to actually see it. The distant flickering lightning contrasted with the growing darkness but did not have the power to illuminate the world around them.

He watched her watching the waves of the lake with her large, dark eyes. The soft breeze gently lifted the loose strands of her black hair from her face. It danced about, taunting him, begging him to reach out and tuck the hair back behind her ear. His eyes followed the curve of her lovely neck down her back to her trim waist. He allowed himself a moment more of watching her breathe, admiring the way her deep, even breaths subtly moved her body.

She was beautiful.

She shifted her weight, bringing him back to himself. With a silent curse at his foolishness, he made a cursory glance across the nearly empty docks.

"My father also told me that sailors who die ashore would rather be returned to the sea than given a proper burial, though that's not what he wants." Her voice was full, thick with emotion.

"Most do, but they generally don't talk about it much. Figure life's too short to worry about dying, I suppose," Miguel said, unable to keep the trace of bitterness from coloring his voice as he watched a passer-by.

"A dear friend of mine died a couple of days ago. We sent him out to sea the night before last from right here." Maria picked at the wood of the rail.

Don Ciro had mentioned that, and he'd wondered when she'd bring it up.

"I do believe I saw you then. *La Solidad* was anchored nearby, and I was on deck. I saw you come and slip something in the water and watch it on its way." He looked at her. "Who was it?"

"My protector and friend."

Ice filled Miguel's stomach like a dunk in the English Channel, and he tightened his grip on the cutlass. "What happened to him?"

"He was in an accident, was run over by a carriage." Maria's voice thickened. "I dreamt of him last night. He stood by me and seemed to say everything would be all right. My father gave me full

72

responsibility for him, and I raised him the best I could. He saved my life at least once, here on this very dock, and now he's gone."

The dog. Relief filled Miguel like coming up for air, and he held back a laugh. *It's just the silly dog.* He put his arm around Maria's shoulders as she sobbed softly. She was so young.

"Come, Maria. Let's get you home." He gently urged her forward and started toward her home.

***

Maria waited alone in the tall grass near the edge of the jungle, but for what, she wasn't sure. A playful breeze pulled at her hair, and tossed it about her shoulders as she looked up at the sunny sky. It ought to be raining; it always rained here. She could see the city off in the distance, could smell the fresh cool scent of the lake mingling with the thick earthy tones of the jungle behind her.

The grass behind her rustled, and Maria spun around. To her surprise and joy, Alistair leapt up at her, nearly knocking her off her feet.

You rascal, you! Maria hugged him as he dropped back to the ground. She playfully knocked his head to the side, tugging on one ear. The large dog seemed to smile as he pushed back, and she fell to the ground, his short, wiry fur rough against her skin.

Maria laughed gleefully as they wrestled until she finally pushed him off and he sat beside her.

You really had me worried that you'd gone, she told him as she rubbed his ears.

He turned and looked at her, a sad little smile in his eyes.

Oh. Maria slumped.

They sat like that for a time, until Alistair stood and began to walk back toward the city.

Where are you going?

He stopped and looked back at her, his head cocked as if to say, *Are you coming?*

She stood as he pranced playfully away, then came loping back. Laughing, she ran toward him and chased him until she woke.

***

"Still dreaming of Alistair?" Betania asked one August afternoon as they lounged in the garden.

"Often enough." Maria returned the stone chess pieces to their box. If she hurried, Elisa might not notice they'd finished and ask for a game. Selena was safely asleep with her embroidery on her lap.

"Think Miguel plays?" Betania settled in the last of her pieces.

"He does, and better than you." Maria smiled, the familiar feeling of warmth in her chest at the mention of her father's assistant.

"What does he do all day, anyway?"

Maria shrugged as a warm breeze fluttered through the trees. "Important things, no doubt."

"And yet he always manages to show up right when you need an escort." Betania gave Maria a look, and Maria laughed.

"It's not like that." Maria shut the box and set it aside. She didn't want to talk about how he made her feel every time she saw him. She didn't really want to think about it, either.

"But you wish it were."

"Am I that obvious?" He was just her father's employee. Certainly her feelings would move on to someone more appropriate with time.

Betania laughed and stood. "No, I'm just that observant."

"You're done?" Elisa said, making Maria jump. "It's my turn against you, Maria. I'll win this time, I'm sure of it."

"Light or dark?" Maria, resigned to her lot, offered Elisa the box. Maybe if Elisa chose her color, she wouldn't whine when she lost this time. Without hesitation, Elisa picked the light pieces and sat, fanning her blue skirt over the seat.

Within minutes, Maria had Elisa cornered three different ways and ready to mate in two moves. Elisa stewed over the pieces, pulling on one of her dangling, blonde curls, while Maria tried to decide if the younger girl would move or knock over the board. How Elisa could be nearing her quinceañera and still have such a wild temper, Maria couldn't fathom.

At the sound of the gate opening, Elisa jumped to her feet to see who had come.

"That's one way to avoid losing, I suppose," Maria muttered to Betania, who merely looked up from her book.

A young page stood just inside the garden gate, fiddling with a pouch in his hands.

"Well?" Elisa snapped at him when he didn't speak. Maria watched the exchange with mild interest. She should probably just call it a forfeit and put the board away.

"Señorita Elisa." The young page's words rushed over each other. "I have been sent with a message for each of the four of you." The boy stood straighter in an attempt to look composed and held out an envelope to Elisa.

She snatched it from him with a sniff and held her hand out for the rest.

Maria felt a pang of sympathy for the poor mestizo boy as he gathered his nerve to speak.

"My instructions were to deliver each one personally."

"Can you not see that they are all here?" Elisa swept her hand toward the others. "They all see you; they heard that you have something for them. Now give them to me and go."

The boy shrank back from Elisa, dropping his gaze to the ground. "I cannot," he said in a small voice.

"I will see you dismissed." Elisa stomped her foot and she held out her hand again.

That's enough of that. Maria stood and strode toward them, knowing what would happen if she didn't intervene.

The page boy again shook his head, and Elisa raised her hand to strike.

"Elisa!" Maria grabbed Elisa's wrist. "What on earth do you think you're doing?"

"Let go of me! This is no affair of yours," Elisa huffed, but she withdrew, throwing the page one last glare before stalking away to a bench, her back to the group.

Maria watched her go. At least the chess game was over.

"What's going on?" Selena's sleepy voice came from the corner.

"This page has messages for us." Maria gestured to the boy and smiled as he handed her the folded paper with her name scrawled elegantly across it. "What is your name?"

"Juan," he answered timidly, his eyes still lowered.

"Thank you, Juan," Maria said with a large, warm smile.

Juan looked up and flashed her a grin of his own before hurrying to Selena and Betania.

"You did the right thing, doing as you were instructed," Betania told him as he handed hers and Selena's to them. "I'll make sure Elisa doesn't cause you trouble for this."

The boy bowed and dashed from the garden, clearly grateful to get out of the situation.

Maria's eyes dropped down to the letter she was holding. It wasn't any handwriting she was familiar with. Who would be writing to all four of them? Intrigued, she opened it.

My Dear Dark-Eyed Angel (Maria),

Maria grinned. Miguel. Why was she not surprised?

You are hereby invited to an evening of fun, food, and ghost stories. The frivolities will commence this very evening. A carriage will arrive at the Casa de la Cuesta at six o'clock sharp to carry yourself and your three companion angels to the secret location.

Your current attire will suffice, but if you or your companions wish to don additional frills, that would be acceptable. There is no need to RSVP (or inform your father, as he has already been apprised of the situation), however you will be asked to provide entertainment during the latter part of the evening in the form of a ghost tale.

You will be returned to your home ~~eventually~~ at a decent hour. I greatly look forward to your presence.

Your servant,

Miguel

Maria's heart warmed to be holding a paper that he had written on. Written her name on, no less. She rolled her eyes at her own reaction and refolded the letter, tucking it safely into a pocket. *Don't be such a fool. He wrote them letters, too.*

"It would appear we have been invited to dinner," Selena said, stretching.

"Oh! How exciting!" Elisa's petulance had evaporated as quickly as it had come. "I know just the story I want to tell!"

"We'd better go get cleaned up." Betania stood demurely, as though to balance her sister's exuberance. "Elisa, stop bouncing so much. You're not a child anymore, and it is not as though it is the first dinner invitation you have ever received."

"Yes, it is." Selena snickered despite her attempts to mimic Betania's composure.

"Hmph!" Elisa stuck her nose in the air. "I'm not even sure I want to go; it seems so drab and boring."

The opportunity was too good to pass up. Maria wadded up a handful of leaves and threw them at Elisa. "You're just worried you'll be frightened by the scary stories."

"I am not." Elisa huffed, flicking the leaves from her dress, but missing one that stuck in her hair.

Maria smirked and began toward the gate, with Elisa following.

"It's not that," Betania said as she and Selena followed suit. "She's just worried that Miguel will think her tales are childish."

"If she can think of any at all," Selena chimed in, stepping a little faster to get ahead of Maria.

"I'll show you all!" Elisa attempted to beat Selena to the gate without breaking into a run. "My story will be the best you've ever heard!"

"Only in your dreams," Maria said, as she and Betania moved to overtake the younger two girls through the gate. Before long, they had left their calm demeanors behind, racing back towards the house without a care in the world.

By a quarter to six, the four girls stood in the loggia beside the front door of the large house, primped, polished, and wearing simple jewelry. Elisa and Selena had done their hair up in semi-elaborate styles. For a time they had entertained the idea of dressing up as silly as they could manage, but, to Maria's relief, better sense prevailed.

A coach pulled around the fountain, stopping before them, and the other three tittered at its obvious age. It was an older style, and lacked much in the way of embellishments, but was obviously well kept. Maria recognized the vehicle immediately as one of her father's. *Now why would he be using that one?* The coach, as was typical of things under the care of Don Ciro, had been well cared for, but they hadn't used it in years. It looked to have been re-outfitted with drapes over the windows and a couple of other decorative touches, as though to disguise it.

Maria also recognized the familiar form of Diego, who had been one of her father's drivers for as long as she could remember. She smiled at him as he pulled the horses to a stop with a soft, "Ho there," and leapt down to open the door. Elisa muttered about a footman as Maria let the other girls in first, giving them their choice of the seats. She nodded to Diego as he helped her in and shut the door behind her, pulling closed the drapes.

"It's all right, you can leave them open," Maria said to him.

"Forgive me, Señorita, but my instructions were to close them." Diego gave her a small bow and retreated to the driver's seat.

"Why do you suppose Miguel needs the blinds closed?" Selena asked as the coach started forward, rocking gently.

"He said the location was secret," Elisa whispered.

"I tend to think he just wants it to be a surprise, don't you think, Maria?" Betania asked.

Maria nodded, her mind on the horses that had been chosen rather than the conversation around her. The horses were an older pair, but well-matched and steady. Like most of Ciro Álvarez's possessions, they were finer than one might initially believe, given their appearance; well-trained, well-used, and well-maintained. But why those two? Her father didn't have a large stable by any means, but he hadn't used Alonzo and Sancho for the carriages for several years, not since he'd purchased the nearly identical chestnuts.

The carriage pulled to a stop only a couple of minutes after they'd started, and Maria shook her head. They were either halfway back to the village or had simply circled around to another spot on the plantation grounds. As she braced herself for the tell-tale rocking of the coach as the driver got down, the door flew open to a chorus of startled gasps.

Chapter 6

"WELCOME SEÑORITAS!" Miguel stood before them, holding the door open. The golden tones of sunset filled the air around them as he held his hand to help her down.

Maria's heart beat a little faster as she set her hand in his. His fingers tightened around hers, warm and firm, as he steadied her while she stepped from the coach. His other hand, under her elbow, seemed to make her world solid in a way it hadn't been before. She looked into his green eyes, his smiling face, and her breath caught in her throat. Before she could get lost in the depths of his eyes, he broke contact, reaching to help Betania.

Desperate to clear her head, she stepped away, glad that she had managed to keep her balance when he let go. She immediately recognized the small grove as one well within the bounds of the de la Cuesta plantation, just out of sight of the house. Maria nearly laughed at the silliness of it. Diego must have taken a long, circuitous route to have made the ride so long. On the other side of the grove stood a small table with a clean, pale tablecloth. The simple yet elegant decorations of local flowers framed the spread of food, punch, and dishware. A fire pit encircled by benches awaited them in the center of the grove.

"Oh, it's lovely!" Elisa exclaimed. Maria turned in time to watch Elisa stepping from the coach, and she could have sworn Elisa misstepped purposefully, toppling into Miguel's arms with an "Oof!"

"Careful." Miguel smiled, swinging her away from the coach, and set her feet carefully on the ground.

"Oh, Miguel! I could have died!" she cried, with her arms still about his neck.

"Not likely with that hard head of hers," Betania muttered to Maria and Selena as they joined her.

"Well, you're safe now." He pulled her arms gently from his neck.

Maria felt a surge of anger well up inside her, but she quickly pushed it back down. Why should she let it bother her? Elisa was just a flirt, and Maria didn't care *that* much about Miguel anyway. Did she?

The coach pulled away and Maria shook her head, making her way to the table. The golden light of sunset gave way to true twilight, and several servants appeared to light the torches that surrounded the clearing.

"It's amazing that it hasn't rained," Maria said to Miguel as he and Elisa came up to them.

"I spoke with the rain gods this afternoon, and they informed me it would be clear all night," Miguel answered solemnly, sliding his arm from Elisa's grasp. "Come, help yourselves to the food. I'll get the fire started."

84

"I'm famished." Selena picked up a plate and delicately added food. The other three followed suit, then took a seat on the benches to watch Miguel attempt to light the fire while they ate.

"Are you sure you know how to build one of those properly?" Selena asked while he moved the wood around in the pit.

"I can't imagine why a sailor would need to know how to build a fire." Elisa took a seat, spreading out her skirt with a flourish.

"Unless he was the ship's cook," Betania offered, sitting beside Maria.

"Potato boy, maybe." Elisa giggled.

"I'll have you know there are many reasons to build a fire when you're a sailor," Miguel said without turning his head from his work.

"I'd like to see that," Maria continued, ignoring his comment. "I can just imagine him swinging that sword of his around to slice the potatoes!"

"The proper name for it is a cutlass," Miguel interjected.

"Back, you fiendish potato!" Selena stood, waving her fork at an imaginary potato as the girls giggled. "Back, I say, or I shall cut you to bits! No? Well, you asked for it! Whack! Whack! Whack!"

Selena straightened haughtily and bowed with a flourish of her fork to the girls' applause. She paused for a beat before grinning and returning to her supper.

"You laugh now, but those potatoes can be awfully dangerous if you let them get out of hand." Miguel rocked back on his heels as the fire flared up before him. "And, while yes, I have cut up my fair share of potatoes, you'll have to guess again. I did not work in the galley or the mess, at least not since I was very young. And I would never use my cutlass on a potato."

"Well, if you didn't travel the seas trying to rid the world of evil potatoes, what did you do?" Betania asked.

Maria's eyes followed him as he rose and went to the table.

"I sailed on a merchant ship." Miguel filled his plate.

Elisa tucked her skirts closer as she watched him from the corner of her eye, making space on her bench, presumably for Miguel.

"I'm not sure that will help any," Maria whispered to Betania, with a nod to Elisa. "There's not enough room on that bench for more than herself, her skirts, and her ego as it is."

"Hush." Betania elbowed her, stifling a giggle.

"It's true though, and you know it." Maria poked her back.

"Did you ever encounter pirates?" Elisa asked, batting her eyes at Miguel.

"Maybe." He walked around the fire, bypassing Elisa to sit on a bench of his own. Maria smiled at Elisa's pout. "But the sailing itself really wasn't very interesting, got kind of monotonous after a while."

"Do you ever miss being at sea?" Selena asked.

"Sometimes." Miguel shrugged. "I miss the beauty of the sunsets and the uncertainty in a storm. Other things."

"What other things?" Elisa asked, returning to the table for a glass of the punch.

"Well," Miguel hesitated, staring at his plate. "Seeing new things," he finished, faltering over his words.

"There are plenty of new things to see here," Selena said as Elisa returned with her glass and sat right next to Miguel.

Betania leaned over to Maria and whispered. "I think he means women."

Maria blushed and nodded her agreement. She hadn't thought about that before. Did he have someone special awaiting his return on some distant shore?

"Tell us about some of the exotic women you've seen," Betania said. "What kind of things do they wear? Do they act very differently from civilized Europeans?"

"Well." Miguel stood, trying to disentangle himself from Elisa without upsetting her drink. "Voyages take a very long time, so while I have been to the other side of the world before, I don't remember much of it. The ship I've been on for the last few years didn't travel to exotic places." He managed to finally slip free of Elisa, and Maria smirked at her perturbed look until Miguel strode up to them. "May I sit between you two angels?" he asked.

"I don't know," Maria whispered loudly to Betania. "Do you really think we should?"

"I mean, would it be safe? I still think he's some sort of potato pirate or something," she replied.

"Potatoes are one thing," Miguel said, lowering his voice and giving them a pleading look, "but I think your sister's amateur attempts for my attention are another."

"I agree. We should take pity on him," Betania concluded, and they moved apart to let him sit.

"I am much obliged to you good ladies." He nodded to them as he sat.

***

The joking and banter continued throughout the meal, punctuated by a round of word games and riddles. The word play fascinated Miguel, giving him insight into his newly adopted language. His father had always said that truly knowing a language was different from being able to speak it.

As the sky darkened, revealing the brilliant stars overhead, the servants removed the remaining food, dishes, and even the tables. From the corner of his eye, he watched Maria's face in the firelight as she looked toward the house with a thoughtful look. What was going through that mind of hers, behind those dark eyes? She wouldn't be able to see the lights of the house through the thick trees. The plan had been to make it seem they were secluded, though the household would certainly be able to see their fire. Don Ciro had loved the plan when Miguel suggested the location.

"Come, let's have some stories!" Selena's voice interrupted Miguel's thoughts.

"I suppose it is late enough." Miguel said, drawing his mind back to the present. "Who should go first?"

"You!" Elisa practically jumped out of her seat with enthusiasm. "I'm sure you have the scariest stories of all, collecting them from all over the world."

"Sure do." Miguel nodded. "But what fun would it be if the best story went first?"

"Are you saying that our stories couldn't possibly be as good as yours?" Maria poked his side. He swatted at her hand, and she moved back, grinning up at him.

"I think that is exactly what he is saying," Selena said. "Who would like to go first, then?"

"I will!" Elisa bounced up and moved to stand opposite the others.

"This is a tale of two young lovers, tragically separated." Elisa began with a note of melancholy in her voice.

"Oh, great," Betania muttered. "Not this one again."

"Once, many years ago, there was a beautiful young princess," Elisa continued, flicking her hair. "And she was in love with a charming prince."

"Of course he'd never be a scoundrel prince," Maria returned quietly to Betania, who snorted.

Miguel smiled, trying not to laugh as they teased the oblivious narrator throughout her story. Selena, however, was as enthralled by Elisa's story as Elisa was in telling it. The story of the two young lovers who had been separated through mischance might have been worth listening to from a better narrator.

"I'm going to guess they both die," Miguel whispered to Maria.

"Careful, she might throw a flaming potato at you for spoiling her story," Maria whispered back.

"It's okay," Betania added, leaning forward to look at Maria. "He's brought his cutlass, he'll be fine."

"Sure, he will be, but what about us? We'll be splattered with bits of flaming potatoes, and then where will we be?"

Several retorts came to mind, and none of them appropriate. Biting his tongue, Miguel reluctantly returned his attention to Elisa's story. Sure enough, the young man died, and the girl waited for him in her garden until she, too, died. They clapped politely while Elisa curtsied with a flourish and returned to her seat. Maria raised an eyebrow at Miguel, asking his opinion of the tale.

"Flaming potatoes aside, seems stupidly tragic to me," he whispered to her, "but I suppose I can see the draw in it for girls."

"So you're saying they don't have such tragic tales of love among sailors?" Betania asked, her voice low as Selena took Elisa's place.

"Sure, or close enough. A better narrator might be able to pull it off, but it's a fool who mopes themselves to death for not getting her way."

Maria nodded, and Selena began.

She surprised them all with a ghost story without a single element of romance. Miguel hadn't thought she had such practicality in her. The tale of a ghost who possessed his still-living friends in his lust for blood and revenge sent a chill through Miguel. He'd heard stories like this before, but sailors tended to be a superstitious lot, and there was always an undercurrent of real fear when such tales were told. In the end, the ghost had succeeded in destroying his friends, both those who had betrayed and those who had helped him, and had been left alone, doomed to wander through the centuries alone in his misery to torment the unfortunate soul who next passed his way.

Selena's voice faded into the night, and Maria was the first to applaud.

"I didn't realize you were such a storyteller," Miguel said as Selena curtsied.

"*Gracias.*" She beamed at the compliment and she returned to her seat. "It's actually a story that was told to me by a friend of my father's the last time they were in port."

"That makes sense, then." Miguel rose to add wood to the fire. "I've heard similar stories in my travels. In fact, I almost picked one such to tell tonight. I'm glad I didn't, though. You told it far better than I would have."

Selena blushed and looked at her hands. "Are you going next, Betania?" she asked, drawing the attention away from her.

"Certainly." Betania stood, taking a moment to brush away non-existent dirt from her skirt and moving with her typical deliberate grace. Taking her place on the other side of the fire, she gazed into the fire, centering herself. What sort of tale had this down-to-earth, quiet young woman brought, Miguel wondered as he returned to his seat beside Maria.

Squaring her shoulders and lifting her head, Betania took a deep breath and began to sing an Italian aria. Her pitch was perfect, and her unaccompanied voice was clear and strong. Given Maria's stunned look, Miguel guessed that she'd never heard her friend sing. Not like this anyway, and he found himself impressed. Betania often sang quietly to herself, as reserved and shy in this as everything else he'd ever seen her do. Listening to her sing, really sing, was something else. There was a strong, powerful personality hidden behind that reserved and quiet exterior.

The final note of her crisp voice hung in the air for a moment after the song ended, mixing with the crackling of the flames. Miguel stood and clapped loudly, breaking the spell. Maria and Selena joined enthusiastically. Betania ducked her head and returned to her seat.

"I didn't know you could sing like that!" Selena exclaimed. "Did you, Elisa?"

"Of course." Elisa crossed her arms and refused to look at her sister. "It wasn't as though it was great or anything."

"You'd have to be deaf to think that wasn't amazing," Miguel said with a laugh, and moved to stoke the fire. Betania blushed again and Elisa snorted as Miguel continued. "I suppose that just leaves Maria."

"Only because you're afraid our stories are better than yours." Maria said, taking her place across the fire.

Miguel returned to his bench, watching her. She moved in a way that was subtly different from the others. He could only describe it as more solid, more true, as though each movement was a deliberate way to say, "This is me."

"This is a story my duenna, Nana, told me long ago."

"This is supposed to be scary stories, not nursery tales," Elisa cut in with a groan.

Without so much as a glance at Elisa, Maria continued. "It is a story about the natives of this land, the Wayuu. They have passed it down, father to son and mother to daughter, through the generations."

Elisa snorted again, and Miguel settled back against the hard bench, excited for a taste of local legend.

"Many generations ago, long before the arrival of the *Conquistadores*, the Wayuu, a free and proud people, were also a peaceful people. One day, a stranger arrived. It is not remembered how he came, whether by ship or some less ordinary means. All that is known is that he came. He appeared on the shore, a young man with skin pale as the moon and hair the color of sand. He moved with speed beyond sight, and with strength enough to crush stones with his bare hands. The people, always friendly, welcomed him. But the elders, who conversed with the spirits of the dead, were wary."

A slight breeze pushed through the small clearing, pushing the smoke toward Maria as she spoke. She stood her ground, and the breeze changed directions, taking the smoke with it.

"The stranger spoke to them with a silver tongue and endless patience. Eventually, much as the elders had feared, the stranger lured the more foolhardy youth from their homes with promises to grant them their hearts' desires. By the time anyone had realized the deception, it was too late, for youth had been enslaved, both body and mind.

"There was nothing anyone could do to free them, nor were the victims able to free themselves. They were in the stranger's complete control."

Miguel could almost see the figures in the fire, caught by things beyond their power. He could sympathize with them. Wasn't that always the way things went? The sage and wise warn the young and foolish to follow the way and be wary of the stranger, and always it ends the same—with the young fool enslaved for following his dream.

"Not many years afterward, another stranger came to them with the same uncanny qualities as the first. This time, the Wayuu were cautious. The newcomer professed to have noble intentions, wishing only to free them from the captor who'd stolen their very lives. Unable to find a better way, the Wayuu agreed to a

94

price that seemed reasonable. With the help of the Noble One, the Slaver was defeated."

And what of the youth that had been enslaved? Miguel tightened his hand on his cutlass. No doubt, destroyed in the crossfire.

"The Noble One remained among them, teaching them new ways to defend themselves. He helped prepare them for further invaders to their land, so that when our people first came here, the Wayuu were not destroyed like many of their cousins. They were not impressed by our pale-skinned ancestors whose speed and strength were that of any ordinary man's. To this day, the Wayuu remember the slavery of the first stranger and continue their fight, for it is said that so long as they remember they will always be free."

Maria fell silent, and returned to her seat.

"That wasn't much of a ghost story," Selena said. "It wasn't even scary."

"Besides, who wants to hear some stupid native legend?" Elisa chimed in. "Everyone knows that someday those savages will be tamed and cultured, the same as all the rest."

"Perhaps they don't want to be." Betania's voice had returned to its typical quiet reticence.

"How could they possibly not want to be?" Elisa asked. "What do they have that is better than what we could give them?"

Try as he might, Miguel could not think of an answer that Elisa would understand. He shook his head and glanced into the shadows beyond the trees. A figure moved through the shadows and gave him a signal. At Miguel's nod, the figure melted back into the darkness. Miguel cleared his throat and stood.

"My turn, I think, señoritas," he interjected into the pause of the conversation, conscious that many of the lingering servants were mestizos, half-breeds between the Spaniards and natives. "Despite all of your concerns, I am not afraid that my tale will fail to live up to yours."

He walked with surety, his familiar jacket swirling about him and his left hand resting lightly on the hilt of his cutlass which swung at his side. He knew well how to radiate the aura that he was a dangerous man, and how to utilize it to good effect. He stopped far enough back from the fire to cast shadows across his face as he smoothed the laughter from it. For the final touch, he ran his hands through his hair, pulling just enough of it loose to frame his face with a casually disheveled look. Taking a deep breath, he began his tale.

"Everything has an origin." He could feel the stillness of the girls watching from across the fire. "Every large tree was once a tiny seed; every roaring river begins as a small spring. So, too, did every legend begin, each having a source from which it springs, each having a seed of truth from which it grew.

"I have traveled the world and heard many, many stories. But I have found that in every place, certain tales resurface over and over again. One such is a tale of a beautiful woman who is part fish and tied to the water." He met Elisa's gaze, holding it as he continued.

96

"Though the type of fish and the body of water differ, as does, occasionally, the fate of the man who finds her. But she is still there. King Arthur's Lady of the Lake, Jason's sirens, Atargatis the mermaid, water nymphs and naiads. Even the Orient has their version, the Ningyo of Japan.

"Another such tale is that of a great flood that overcame the Earth," Miguel continued, moving his gaze to Selena when Elisa finally broke eye contact. "In the Christian world, we know it as the flood of Noah, but for Egypt, the world began with a flood from which the first queen of Egypt arrived. In Greek mythology, Zeus sent a flood and killed almost every living man but a few who escaped to high mountains. The Hindus tell a tale of Manu, the first man, who saved a fish, and the fish warned him of the deluge to come and to build a ship, then the fish guided the boat to a safe place. There are many, many more examples, but these are not the tales I wish to share tonight.

"Tonight, I will tell you of another legend that spans the globe." He released Selena and turned his intense stare to Betania, who wouldn't meet his eyes. "Perhaps it even shares its origins with Selena's ghosts and Maria's strangers. It is a tale of a creature who feeds off the very lives of the living—a drinker of blood.

"Now, as I said before, the tales of the blood-drinkers span both history and the globe, from Kali in India, to Sekhmet of Egypt, to the Jiang Shi of the Orient. The most common name for such creatures here in the West is ..." Miguel paused, locking eyes with Maria, and dropped his voice. "... *vampire.*"

Elisa and Selena gasped, and Betania shuddered a little at the word. Maria watched him, meeting his gaze with an intensity of her own.

"I am certain each of you have heard before tales of these demons." Miguel broke eye contact with her before it could distract him. Keeping his voice low and haunting, he continued. "But it is easy to disbelieve stories that happened generations ago. No, my story tonight happened not so long ago, in our very lifetimes, in fact.

"The year was 1725 in the village of Metwett. It was a nice village, as such things go. And though the people were poor, struggling in the aftermath of the recent wars, they were happy. There was one man, Arnold Paule, who had been sent there as a *hajduk*, a militiaman to protect the borders during periods of peace." Miguel swung his cutlass from its sheath and saluted in a smooth and practiced motion. The girls' startled gasps made him grin. He flourished the sword a moment, then returned it to its sheath.

"He was charismatic and friendly and the villagers took to him quickly. There was a tale he loved to tell to anyone who would listen. He claimed that he had once been attacked and bitten by a vampire, infected by its evil. However, due to his quick wits and extreme courage, he had cured himself of its deadly taint by eating the soil from its grave and smearing himself with the corpse's blood." Here, Miguel stooped down and grabbed a handful of warm dirt, letting it slip through his fingers.

"The villagers, considering themselves to be grounded and sensible people, refused to believe such wild, nonsensical tales. But then ... something happened." Miguel dropped the remaining dirt and began a slow circuit around the fire.

"One day, as Arnold Paule helped a neighbor bring in a harvest of hay, he suffered a mishap. No one knows quite how it happened, but Paule fell from the wagon and broke his neck, dead as a nit. Terribly unfortunate, the people thought. But that was all they thought about it, and Paule was buried with due ceremony.

"That, however, was not that. Not three days after his funeral, an old woman walking home from the market saw him standing by the side of the road, beckoning to her." He reached his arm out to Selena, who recoiled. He grinned and continued on. "Startled, the woman walked faster, pretending she had not seen him. But Paule was not to be deterred. He followed swiftly and silently behind her until she reached the safety of her home. He continued to harass her each night, waiting just outside her home for her to come out. By the end of the week, she had begun to go mad with fear and went out to face the revenant."

Miguel stooped to pick up a branch, pausing as he returned to his starting point on the far side of the fire. Crouching down, he poked at the fire and continued. "She was found dead the next morning, with bite marks on her neck and entirely drained of blood. By the end of the month, three more had died in the same manner.

"Scared, the villagers sought the advice of Paule's commanding officer, a foreigner who had seen such things before. He led them in the opening of Paule's grave, and can you imagine what they found?" Miguel paused and stared into darkness beyond the fire, watching the girls shift in the periphery.

"When they opened the grave of Arnold Paule, a full month after he had broken his neck, they indeed found his body. But rather than a dead and rotted corpse, they found it fresh, and far healthier-looking than Paule had ever been in life." Miguel rose slowly, his eyes still downcast toward the fire. "His mouth"— Miguel ran his hands over his own lips—"was covered in fresh blood, dripping down onto his shirt. His nails and skin, regrown. Certain now that Paule had, after all, become a vampire, they drove a stake into his heart." Here Miguel slammed his stick into the center of the fire, and a shower of sparks rose around it. He lowered his voice again and continued. "And Paule? He groaned once more as the latest, fresh blood from his victims oozed out from the wound."

The silence that followed drew on for a moment before Elisa asked breathlessly, "What happened then?"

Miguel shrugged and in his regular voice said, "They burned his body, and, for good measure, gave the same treatment to his four victims."

"Did that stop the killings?" Selena asked, shivering in the darkness.

100

"Until the next vampire came," Miguel said with a careless gesture.

"Are you going to tell us about that one, too?" Betania asked.

"Nope; you all told only one story tonight, and so did I." Miguel rolled his shoulders and looked up at the moon advancing across the sky. "Besides, it's far too late for any more tonight, I think."

He returned to his seat between Maria and Betania as the girls began their typical chatter. Except for Maria, who watched the flames dancing in the darkness.

"What do you see?" she asked Miguel after a moment.

"See? Do you mean aside from the dark-haired angel before me?" he teased.

Maria laughed and gestured toward the dwindling fire. "No, I mean in flames. Do you ever look at them and imagine they're alive?"

"Sometimes." He looked at the flames, moving like wisps of thoughts, insubstantial as the passing of moments. "There is something about a fire in the darkness that I think most people are drawn to, in one way or another."

"I like to watch them dance. When I watch long enough, they seem like little faeries flitting to music only they can hear." A gentle breeze pulled loose a lock of her hair, which Maria tucked behind her ear.

Miguel nodded and stared into the flames. "The fae are often thought to be seen in the flames. Some people like to imagine the future when they look, and others only see the past."

They lapsed into silence, though he thought she might ask which he saw. Just as she seemed to have gathered the courage to ask, the coach returned to the clearing, and the moment was lost. He looked up to Diego, the driver. Meeting his eyes, Diego gave a tight smile. All was clear. Relief washed through him as a tension he'd been ignoring dissipated. Standing and straightening his jacket, he cleared his throat to get the girls' attention.

"Well my angels, it appears to be fairly late," Miguel announced, his voice chipper. "It is definitely past time I returned you all to the safety of your homes."

Giggling and teasing each other, including a scream from Elisa when Selena poked her side, the four girls allowed Miguel to help them back into the coach. Miguel pulled himself up beside the driver, and they took the direct route back to the Casa de la Cuesta. After dropping off the Señoritas de la Cuesta with their cousin, Miguel joined Maria inside the cabin. He sat across from her, hoping she might restart their conversation, but she watched thoughtfully out the window. After a minute or two, he settled back, his right hand resting on the butt of his pistol just inside his jacket, and closed his eyes to listen to the familiar creak of the carriage.

Chapter 7

OCTOBER 1739 - MARACAIBO

MARIA LISTENED with half an ear to the chatter of the girls as they sat in the drawing room of Casa de la Cuesta, droning on like the buzzing of insects as they patched old clothes to give to the poor. The skin on her neck itched with the sweat that lay on it, and she wished she could flick her ear like a horse to dislodge the noise. Instead, she patted her damp neck with a handkerchief. Not that it would do any good, of course. Maria set her stitching on her lap and stretched her shoulders discreetly. The hot season was not her favorite time of year, but, thank goodness, it would be over soon. She'd probably have been less wet if she'd jumped in the lake. Now that was an idea. Really, anything was better than spending all afternoon sewing.

Without warning, Elisa jumped up from her darning, startling Maria and silencing the other girls.

"We should have a ball!" Elisa clapped her hands.

"Took you all day to think of that?" Betania muttered, turning back to her stitches.

"I'm serious! The weather will be turning soon, so it would be cool enough to dance all night." Elisa still stood, a gleeful gleam in her eye.

"A ball would take months to put together," Betania objected.

"So let it take months." Elisa's voice turned pleading.

"We'd need to host it here," Selena said.

"Of course it would need to be here," Elisa said with a laugh. "Where else could it be? It's not as though the ballroom at the Álvarez's provincial little *hacienda* could hold a real ball. It would be perfect here!"

Maria let the slight against her home slide. They had a perfectly serviceable ball room at the *hacienda*, even if it wasn't as grand as the Casa de la Cuesta. Really, Maria wanted to contradict her just because of the obnoxious tone, but a ball did sound fun.

"It could be a masked ball." Selena kept her voice small.

"Yes! We could invite everyone in Maracaibo–" Elisa started.

"No," Maria cut her off, resuming her stitches. She could feel their eyes on her, but she remained stoic.

"No?" Elisa asked with a pout. "Why ever not?"

Maria raised her eyes and gave them a coy smile. "Not everyone in Maracaibo, but perhaps a masked ball for all the eligible young men and young ladies."

"With sufficient chaperones, of course." Betania lowered her stitches and a grin grew on her face.

"Of course!" Elisa bounced about and pulled Betania to her feet.

"If we time it right we could have it outside, in one of the gardens," Selena said breathlessly. Elisa pulled her to her feet as well.

"We'll have to make a guest list, and plan out flower arrangements and what kind of food we should have! Oh, there's so much to plan!" Elisa was set to bounce right off the balcony if she didn't rein in her excitement a little. "Can you imagine? A ball at the Casa de la Cuesta! Hosted by the four of us! None will have ever seen the like!" Elisa's face was aglow with the vision in her head.

"There's only one problem, Elisa." Maria said, genuinely hating to be the bearer of bad news in this case. "We'll have to clear it with your mother."

The girls slumped back down into their chairs.

"It might not be as grand," Maria offered into the silence, "but I'm sure my father would allow it at our home if she turns us down."

Elisa scoffed. "Who would want to go to a ball hosted by a merchant's daughter, Maria? Really? Besides, I'm sure mother won't tell us no."

"Elisa," Betania chided, shocked.

Maria had it on the tip of her tongue to tell Elisa she wouldn't be invited if she found the *hacienda* so *provincial* when Doña Olivia's voice came from the doorway.

"What will I not tell you no about?" Doña Olivia stood in the doorway with her hands planted on her hips.

Maria and Selena looked at Elisa, who looked pleadingly at Betania, who stared at the floor before her feet.

"Well?" Doña Olivia prodded after a moment with a hint of a smile in her voice. As it wasn't her idea, Maria felt no need to speak up. Besides, if Doña Olivia turned them down, she could always approach her father.

Finally, Betania squared her shoulders and looked at her mother.

"Mother," she started firmly, and Maria gave her a sharp look. She'd never spoken so boldly about anything. "Maria, Selena, Elisa, and I have decided to host a masked ball. We would be pleased to hold it at the Casa de la Cuesta, with your permission."

Selena and Elisa gaped at Betania's request, but Maria couldn't help feeling proud of her friend. Certainly Selena was the most timid, but Betania had never shown any sort of backbone to anyone. Anyone she perceived to be her better, at any rate, and that certainly included her formidable mother.

Unaccountably, Doña Olivia smiled. "I've often felt of late that the Casa de la Cuesta has been quiet for far too long. Your quinceañeras aside, the last real party we held here was just after Elisa was born, a few years after we arrived. I can hardly believe it has been so long. Tell me, girls, what are your plans?"

She took a seat and sent a servant for a pen, ink and paper. Selena took notes as they schemed. For the most part Doña Olivia let them make all the decisions, though she pointed out potential problems and overruled things that were too outrageous.

In the end, they settled for an evening in January, though the girls had hoped for a Yule ball, when the rain would be least likely and the evening decently cool. With instructions to create a guest list, Doña Olivia sent them out to their garden.

The humidity in the garden wasn't much better than it had been in the house, but as the task was far less dull, Maria didn't mind it as much. They sat along the side of the small pond, their feet in the water as they giggled more than discussed who should be invited and who should not.

"Rosalina Garcia Arce definitely needs to come."

"Yes, but not her sister Juana, she's so snobbish!"

"Well, we can't very well invite the one without the other," Betania mediated.

"Very well, we won't invite either," Elisa said.

"What about their older brother, Benito? He's too gorgeous to not invite," Betania said.

"I suppose his beauty might make up for his sisters." Maria shrugged, fiddling with a wreath of flowers she'd been braiding.

"Not to mention how graceful he is at the dance." Betania looked wistfully into the pond.

"And just how would you know?" Elisa demanded.

"She couldn't take her eyes off of him at last year's Yule celebration." Selena snickered as she wrote down the names.

"I remember now! He asked her to stand with him in a dance, but she was too tongue-tied to answer him." Maria laughed as Betania blushed.

"Well, this year I shall be old enough to go, and you can bet you won't see me standing alone," Elisa said.

"Now remember, we mustn't tell anyone about this until the invitations are sent." Selena looked pointedly at Elisa, who had the good grace to blush.

"Like Mother said, also, we really must be sure to send an invitation to every family so that none feel snubbed," Betania said. "After all, Papa does business with nearly every respectable family in Maracaibo."

"And all the rest belong to Don Álvarez!" Elisa tossed a posy Maria's way.

Maria stiffened as she caught the flowers. "And just what are you implying, Señorita de la Cuesta?"

"She was just poking a little fun," Betania said quietly.

"Really, Maria, it was just a bit of fun. We all know your father doesn't deal with riff-raff," Elisa began, almost sounding sincere. "Even if he is just a merchant."

"Though he has taken to hiring sea dogs!" Selena put in merrily, oblivious to the change in mood.

"You're right. All of you." Maria's voice was dangerously calm to hide her anger, drawing each of their eyes to her as she stood. "My father is an honest man. He lives off the work of his own hands rather than other men's stolen backs." Elisa turned red at the reference to the slaves that worked her father's plantation, but Maria continued, turning her anger toward Selena. "And at least my father had the decency to stay and take care of his daughter when life dealt him a blow, rather than foisting her off on his in-laws and running back to sea."

Selena's eyes widened in shock and hurt, and Betania put her arms around her.

Shaking with fury, Maria replaced her stockings and shoved her feet into her shoes, her trembling fingers barely able to tie the laces. Clenching her jaw to keep from saying more, she straightened and headed for the gate.

As she opened the heavy, wrought iron grill she heard Betania call softly after her, "At least we all know who our mothers are."

Tears blurred Maria's vision as she fled.

She ran blindly down the way, away from the plantation, when something quite solid knocked her onto her backside. She was grateful it had been dry enough lately that the road wasn't all mud. With a groan, she looked up to see what she'd run into, only to be blinded by the sun.

"I knew angels could fly, but I didn't realize the use of said wings blinded them," a lovely voice said from the sun as hands gently helped her to her feet.

She fumbled around for a moment, straightening her skirt and hair and drying her tears on the proffered handkerchief before turning to her helper.

It was Miguel.

For a moment she couldn't move. She couldn't breathe. Then, as if taking all the time in the world, he reached to her face. She turned her face toward him, closed her eyes and ....

Time slammed back into motion as he tucked a lock of hair behind her ear and picked a leaf from her shoulder. She turned away from him for a moment, took a deep breath to compose herself, and then looked back with a smile.

Her smile nearly broke his heart. What had she just gone through to have a smile so filled with sorrow? Glancing toward the house, Miguel made eye contact with the servant who had been following her. The woman gave no indication that anything was amiss, so he nodded a dismissal, and the woman turned back to the house.

"Really, for a man who claims to have lived so long at sea, you do an amazing impression of a very large rock," she said lightly, though her voice was still thick from her tears. With a quick look over Maria to assure himself that she was unharmed, Miguel simply chuckled and offered his arm. She took it and set a brisk pace away from the Casa de la Cuesta.

An anger inside him demanded to know who had upset her so he could return and teach them manners. *Not that she'd appreciate such a thing.* He smiled. It

110

wasn't really the smartest thing to do anyway. Besides, he was Don Ciro's man, and his actions reflected on his employer. And on his employer's daughter. Miguel stood a little straighter as they walked.

As they neared the town Miguel decided he'd given her enough time.

"So, truly, what onerous creature were you running from today?" he asked.

"Not onerous, perhaps, but certainly a terrible monster. With three heads." Maria tried to sound nonchalant, but a quaver remained in her voice.

"Shall I return and slay it for you?" Miguel offered, pulling his cutlass part of the way out with his free hand.

"No, it is far too dangerous a territory for one such as yourself." Maria cracked a smile.

It lifted his heart. Closing his eyes, he steeled himself. She made him happy, but he shouldn't let it be more. He could not get overly attached to his employer's daughter.

"But your father would be most displeased if he ever found out you were going into danger that I knew of but didn't protect you from," Miguel said, coloring his voice with mock hurt. *Actually, he'd probably kill me.*

"Ah, Miguel. The only way to save me from this would be to pack me up and take me some place where no one knew me. Or my father."

"Are you certain that's the *only* way?" Miguel swallowed. The warmth of Maria's hand on his arm suddenly became far more noticeable.

"Either that or remove all the women from my life. Especially the short blond ones." Maria managed a charming smile and batted her eyes at him.

He could smell the warm floral scent she wore, that of an unknown flower that reminded him of the sky at twilight.

"Ah, my lady doth ask much of me." Miguel moved away to give her a wild and deep bow, flourishing his hands. The momentary separation did nothing to clear his head. "I think, of the two tasks lain before me, the former would be the nobler." He paused and, winking, added in a loud whisper, "Not to mention the easier!"

Maria's face brightened as she laughed. "Truly, Miguel, where did you learn such silly things? And for heaven's sake, why?"

Miguel straightened and smiled back at her. "Truly, Maria, anywhere I could. As for the why, well, every man must keep some secrets from the ladies, else we would cease to be mysterious. But, for now, let's say it was so that I could make a dark, lovely angel smile and hear her charming laugh." Miguel again offered his elbow.

"Fair is fair. We can say that for now." Maria took his arm in hers and continued on their walk. He could fight all he wanted, but the weight of her hand on his arm could not be denied. She steadied him, and seeing

112

her happy filled him like wind in a sail. *Just admit it already.* He sighed inwardly, braced himself for the turmoil it would cause in his life, and looked over at the young woman walking beside him. *All right, fine. I am fond of her.*

They lingered in town, ducking into shops or under awnings at the occasional spurt of rain, and talked of unimportant things. Music of one sort or another hung on the air at nearly every corner as the day wound down and twilight fell over the town.

"I dreamt of Alistair again last night," Maria said after a lull in their conversation.

"Was it the same dream you've had before?" Miguel asked, enjoying her nearness and the sound of her voice.

"Sort of. We were standing in the fields outside the city, the wind blowing across the grass. Normally, he would just come up to me, and we'd be together, but last night he started growling." Maria looked up at him. "What do you suppose it means?"

"I don't suppose it means anything more than that you miss your friend," Miguel shrugged.

"I don't know. It's been months since he died, and even though I'm still sad sometimes, I've come to terms with it." Maria pulled him to the side, out of the way of a lamp-lighter. "Maybe it means something is coming."

"Or maybe he's just mad at Elisa for upsetting you." Miguel gave her a playful push as they walked.

She smiled up at him, but shivered as an unseasonably cool wind blew in from across the coast.

"I wish I'd brought a shawl," she said absently, rubbing her arms.

Miguel shrugged out of his coat and draped it over her shoulders. She pulled it close around her and inhaled his scent, enjoying the lingering warmth. He had newer coats but had found that none of them fit or moved quite as well as this one. A movement out of the corner of his eye caught his attention, and he turned his head casually.

"We should go watch the lightning by the lake," she said with an impish grin. "I'll race you to the docks."

The shadow turned into two men who ducked down an alley leading to the lake.

"It is getting quite late." Miguel shook his head, all playfulness gone from his voice. He took her hand more firmly in his arm and began to walk.

"What is a little darkness?" Maria returned playfully, tugging his arm toward the lake, but she couldn't move his solid frame. Was she trying to get herself hurt?

"And you are in danger of a chill," Miguel said just as seriously as before, steering her down a well-lit street toward her home. He glanced across the street at a burly man who waited, half concealed by a cart. The same man he had seen at least three times in the last hour.

"What is a little chill air on an evening as pleasant as this?" Irritation colored her voice as she shrugged off his arm and turned back toward the lake.

Miguel bit back his own frustration at her childish stubbornness. He could pick her up and throw her over his shoulder, but it would severely hamper his ability to fight if it came to that.

"Maria, I must insist. It is late, and your father will be waiting for us." He took her elbow firmly in one hand and set his other on the small of her back, again aiming her down the brighter street. His every sense became alert, scanning the quickly emptying street for threats.

She jerked her arm out of his grip and turned on him. "My father won't mind a few more minutes, and besides, you're in no position to tell me what to do."

Miguel's full attention snapped to her, and he gave her a stony glare. He could see it, the moment Maria became aware of the silence that filled the street. She hesitated a moment longer, fear warring with anger on her face. Holding her head up, she allowed him to lead her down the brighter street.

Finally. Miguel scowled. *She's come to her senses.* Maria cast a glare up at him as he held her hand tightly in his elbow. *Correction,* he thought, *not sensibility. Pride.* He had better things to worry about just now than her pride. At least she was cooperating.

His free hand rested on the pistol at his hip as the burly man followed. Miguel sped up, and she matched his pace with a small sound of disgust.

As they neared the edge of town and the homes became increasingly distant from each other, their tail fell behind before disappearing completely. Miguel relaxed his grip on her arm a little, though his pace remained hurried.

"Miguel, what—!" Maria started angrily, but Miguel shushed her, gritting his teeth.

Save your breath in case we need to run, he scowled silently. The girl had no sense in her head. He almost wished they had horses.

Maria opened her mouth again as they walked.

Miguel shot her a glare, and whatever protest she'd been about to make remained unspoken. He continued without breaking his stride, but he could feel her fuming beside him.

The Álvarez *hacienda* came into view, and Miguel fought the urge to bolt for the safety of the walled estate. Slowing them to a more deliberate pace, he again tightened his grip on Maria's arm. She tried to jerk away, but he refused to let go. What better place to surprise a person than within sight of safety?

Nothing moved in the shadows, and Miguel forced his lungs into slow, even breaths. Straining his ears over the sound of his own heartbeat, he listened to the silence behind them. As they neared the small side gate, it swung silently open, and they were through. Miguel pushed Maria behind him as he turned to secure the gate, and the watcher who had opened it for them returned to his post.

The solid sound of the gate's latch sliding home released the tension in his chest, even as Maria jerked free from his grasp. Now that she was safe, he let her go, turning to see the burning fury in her dark eyes as his jacket dropped to the ground between them.

"How dare you treat me like that, Miguel!" She glared at him as a gentle rain began to fall.

Miguel picked up his coat and looked at her in stony silence for a moment, closing himself off. "I haven't the slightest idea what you mean," he said flatly and turned to walk away.

She grabbed his elbow, and he reluctantly turned back to face her.

"You know exactly what I mean. Dragging me around, hustling me about as though you were ashamed to be seen with me!"

"Maria!" a loud voice boomed, cutting her off from further accusations.

Miguel snapped up straight as Maria startled at the sight of her father striding toward them through the rain.

"Don Álvarez. M'lady," Miguel said crisply, bowing slightly to them both before striding to the house. The rain was not enough to obscure the voices behind him.

"Well?" Ciro demanded, his usual patient tone entirely gone. "Can you account for yourself? Choosing to so abuse my assistant and our guest?"

"*I* abuse *him*?" Maria demanded. "He pulled me through the streets like, like … well, it was undignified!"

"From what I saw, he escorted you home, safely I will add, and protected you from your own folly of staying out too late."

"I was with him all afternoon! It is every bit his fault that we were out late as it was mine!"

Of course she would blame me. Another stone added to the wall Miguel was building around himself.

"Maria, listen to me. Miguel is a good man whom I trust, and I need you to trust him like you trust me. In the future, you are to do as he tells you." Ciro's voice was firm.

"But Papa! He's so rude and conceited. Especially after tonight, I don't believe I will ever be able to bring myself to speak to him again!"

What a fool he was. He was nothing to her but her father's hired hand. Miguel held his head higher and refused to look back as he opened the door to the house as the rain began to fall in earnest.

"You listen to me, *chica,*" Ciro said, but what he had to say beyond that was lost to Miguel as the door closed behind him.

Chapter 8

T HE CACOPHONOUS cry of gulls filled the air as
Miguel followed Don Ciro to the warehouse. The
sun shone hot on their backs, and Miguel found himself
almost grateful they were on horseback. He'd not have
enjoyed walking so far in this heat. Next time, he would
find some place cooler to stop. Or at the very least, less
humid. Miguel rubbed at the sweat on his neck with his
sleeve. Not that it did any good.

The thought of leaving pulled at him. His initial
agreement with Don Ciro had nearly come to an end,
but after the debacle with his daughter, Don Ciro had
commended Miguel's vigilance and offered him an
early release. Miguel shifted in his saddle, trying to
work sensation back into his knees. In the moment,
Miguel's pride had kept him from accepting, but now
he wasn't as sure. His horse, as though in response,
moved closer to the trees that lined the road, bashing
Miguel's knee. How would it be to be back on the open
ocean? The wind on his face and the vast unknown laid
out before him? *And no beautiful young women to
confuse you or not speak to you for weeks.*

"Do you suppose life is any simpler there?" Maria's question sounded in his mind, and he shook his head as though to dislodge her voice. Without her around every day to complicate things, it certainly would be simpler. Leaving had an allure, but the specter of his father's disapproval hung over him. He scowled. It wasn't as though breaking his contract with Don Álvarez would damage the family name. His uncle ….

Miguel cut off that line of thought. His father was gone, and what was done was past. Maria, on the other hand, was not. He stretched in his saddle as Don Ciro pulled to a stop.

Miguel shoved aside his thoughts of the girl. He needed to focus. "Tell me again why you continue to do business with this man," he asked as he dismounted.

His sable gelding turned to nip at him as his feet touched solid ground. Miguel's legs still protested this new form of transportation, and his stomach felt queasy at the thought of trusting such a large and powerful creature with a mind of its own. He did his best to ignore them both. It was a new skill to learn, and he would do so without regard for fear or pain.

"Still nervous of the horse, Miguel?" Don Ciro clapped Miguel on the shoulder.

The gelding jerked his head away at the motion, and Miguel jumped back, his heart thumping. Don Ciro laughed.

"I'll get over it," Miguel deliberately stepped toward the horse, gently pulling its head back down, and handed him over to Dom, Don Ciro's steward. "You didn't answer my question."

"Maybe I was avoiding it." Ciro straightened his jacket as Dom took the three horses, giving Miguel a look that said, *Nice try*.

"Let me ask you this." Don Ciro led Miguel around to the front of the warehouse. "In all your years aboard a merchant ship, did your captain never take on cargo from a less than perfect vendor?"

"Of course he did, but I don't know that they had ever wanted to kill us, either."

"But say they did. Say you feared he planned to put pox on your ship intentionally. How would you stop him?"

Miguel gripped his cutlass as they neared the doors, rubbing his thumb over the pommel. Killing the man wouldn't solve anything, not that he'd consider that an option anyway. His grip on the weapon tightened. He knew plenty of people who would think it a great solution.

Deliberately, he dropped his hand and forced his muscles to relax, noting his surroundings at the same time. The sun glared off the nearby lake, the breeze from across the water moved gently through the ever present foliage, and the street bustled with sailors and other folk going about their business. Dom and the horses followed behind.

"Not accepting merchandise from him wouldn't be enough," Miguel said, thoughtful. "It'd be a simple thing to sabotage your ship. Bad food, a turncoat on the crew ...."

"Or even pay off a harbormaster to declare your shipment diseased and burn your whole ship and all the wares." Ciro nodded as he pulled open the doors. "So, how do you keep him invested in your well-being?"

Ciro stepped into the dark warehouse without hesitation. Miguel followed a step behind, his sword hand itching to draw. He hated the way Don Ciro strode into situations without bothering to assess them first.

"You're late!" a voice, nasally and arrogant, called from the warehouse's gloom. "I see you've brought your little protégé along. Feeling old are you, Ciro?"

Miguel blinked at the darkness, hoping to adjust his vision more quickly. Shapes began to form, and subtle shifts of movement in his periphery put him on guard. For a moment, he wished he kept the wall to his back, but Don Ciro continued forward and Miguel had to follow.

"Not today, Antonio." Don Ciro grasped the hand and arm of a slender man, giving him a firm handshake. Miguel had never actually seen Gonza before, but the way he grinned back at Don Ciro like a dog baring its teeth, fit exactly with what he'd heard.

After a moment of silent battle between the two merchants, Miguel cleared his throat. The shapes around them had, by now, resolved into crates of merchandise and at least six other men.

"Yes, well." Gonza released his grip and stepped away from Don Ciro. He waved his right hand in a careless gesture, but a glint of motion from the left caught Miguel's eye. Would Gonza really have knifed Don Ciro, given the chance?

"I assume you wish to inspect everything yourself. Here is a copy of the manifest for you." With a quick gesture of Gonza's hand, a skinny boy Miguel hadn't noticed scampered over to him with a leather portfolio. Gonza handed it to Don Ciro and stepped back while Ciro opened it. The two men began their circuit of the warehouse, and Miguel watched the boy. Eight perhaps. Maybe ten. The boy followed Gonza with his eyes, doing his best to mimic the man's gait and stance. He even did a decent job with the haughty expression.

Keeping his breath deliberately calm in hopes to slow his racing heartbeat, Miguel chose to keep his distance from the two merchants as they made their way through the manifest. Of the six men he'd noted, four were working, actually moving crates while the other two merely seemed to work. Miguel made a show of tucking his coat back to more fully reveal the battered cutlass sheath, his hand casually draped over the pommel. *I know you're there*, it said. *You don't want to try it today.*

When Don Ciro and Gonza finally finished, they nodded to each other and again shook hands. Don Ciro led the way to the door, and Miguel gave one last look around, noting the locations of all eight of Gonza's men. He took a step or two backwards, following Don Ciro until he was satisfied that none of the men were close enough to jump on him with a knife before turning and following his employer out the door.

His back itched with the anticipation of a blow even as they stepped into the bright sunlight and Dom handed back the reins of the gelding. Miguel rolled his shoulders and glanced back at the gaping door of the warehouse before mounting up. Don Ciro nudged his horse into a trot and Miguel matched his pace, his hands tight on the reins to keep them from trembling.

"Don Ciro," Miguel called out as they passed out of the docks. "Would he really have knifed you in his own warehouse?"

"Antonio Gonza?" Don Ciro nodded. "Given the chance, without a moment's hesitation."

A weight settled into Miguel's guts. Name or no name, Miguel wouldn't be able to live with himself if he left Maria exposed to a man like that. No matter how it might hurt. Miguel looked up into the sky, noting the storm clouds edging their way in. *Well, Father, at least I got to keep something of yours. Let's just hope our overdeveloped sense of loyalty doesn't get me killed, too.*

***

The rain struck heavily outside Maria's window and she watched it, her fingers in the decorative grate of the window and her forehead resting against it. She longed to get out. To get away from all the watching eyes judging her. But she was nothing if not true to her word. She didn't care what they thought; she had said she wouldn't speak to Miguel, and so she hadn't. Even this morning when he'd greeted her, she had not even acknowledged it. Her father's disapproving look had cut, but she'd steeled herself against it.

At first, it seemed her plan would work. Miguel had been quiet and standoffish with everyone, especially Elisa. The little opportunist had pounced on him as soon as she'd realized she and Miguel weren't talking. Maria scowled at the leaves that refused to be beat down by the rain. But then he had started being *cheery* again. Now he listened to Elisa's prattle.

"Scowling about it won't stop the rain," Nana said from where she stood dusting the shelves.

"I don't know who he thinks he is!" Maria pushed off from the window grate and stalked across the room.

"Do you ever really know who another person is?" Nana said, unperturbed by Maria's outburst.

Maria ignored the comment. "He just goes on as though I'm not even there; talking to Elisa and the others as though he's known them forever. *I* was the one who suggested he speak to my father about a job."

"The del Mar boy again, is it?" Nana said flatly as Maria turned sharply and headed back the way she'd come.

"If not for *me* he'd have probably ended up working as a stable hand and sleeping in a hot, moldy hay loft."

"You would prefer that, would you?" Nana rolled her eyes and set down the duster. "Get over and help me with the bedding."

With more force than necessary, Maria tore the pillows from their covers. "What an ingrate! Then, when it suits him, he orders me around, willy-nilly, and expects me to do what I'm told. And Papa agrees!"

Nana gave her a bland smile.

"Don't you do that." Maria threw the pillow at Nana, who caught it and dropped it into a clean case. "Don't you smile at me like you think I'm wrong. I'm not."

Nana shrugged and began to hum, that same infuriating smile on her face. Maria scowled and continued to help with the bedding. Any other of the household's servants would have been scandalized, or insulted, or both. But Nana had helped raise her, instilling in Maria an almost reflexive desire to work beside her. And, to Maria's chagrin, working always helped calm her temper.

She returned to her window and looked out at the rain as Nana moved on, pretending to straighten the room. Her father's words from the night she'd been unceremoniously dragged home from the docks ran through her mind. He'd given her, in no uncertain terms, the directive to follow Miguel's instructions in the future. As much as it galled her, she would obey her father. Her pride would allow nothing less. But it was the other part that had stung.

I had expected Doña Olivia could teach you to be a woman of sense and had hoped you would manifest at least some of the qualities and goodness of your mother, but I suppose I shall have to make do with the ill-mannered girl you choose to remain.

Maria sniffed, dabbing at the tears that formed in her eyes. She wouldn't cry, even if her father's disappointment hurt like a knife in her heart. How could he compare her to her mother when he wouldn't even talk about her? How was she supposed to measure up to some unknown person? She wanted to be like her mother, to make her father proud, but how could she when he kept so much about her a secret?

Nana's humming stopped abruptly, and began again, this time in a haunting, vaguely familiar tune that toyed with memories just beyond Maria's ability to recall. She looked over at the older woman. Perhaps she could wheedle something more from her?

"Tell me about my mother, Nana," Maria asked.

"What is it that you are wanting to know?" the old woman asked cautiously, setting down the figurine she had been polishing and taking a seat at the table beside Maria.

"Anything. Everything. I don't know anything about her. Father rarely talks about her, and no one else I've met even knows who she was." Maria leaned forward, looking earnestly into Nana's dark brown eyes.

"And why should I be any different?"

"Because you knew her, even better than Papa. You said yourself that you were her nurse, too, when she was a child. Surely you can tell me *something* about her. Papa wouldn't need to know."

Nana held Maria's gaze for a moment longer before settling back into her chair with a thoughtful smile. "Well, now. Ayelen. What to say about her? She was shorter than you as an adult, but you look very much like her with your dark hair and the shape of your eyes. It no doubt pains your father when he looks at you, seeing his beloved wife every time."

"Except when I talk. Or make a decision, or do anything at all." Maria didn't even try to keep the bitterness from her voice. "I know all that. Tell me what she was like."

"She was very sweet and soft-spoken, but she was a woman who knew what she wanted out of life. Very determined. When she set her mind to something, she found a way to get it, always intent on no one getting hurt in the process." Nana straightened the lace on the table. "Why do you ask?"

Maria hmphed, and turned back to the window to hide the hurt in her eyes. "Papa says I'm a shame to him, nothing like her. That I'm just a foolish, selfish girl who could never grow into some half-remembered ideal." Her voice cracked as she continued. "How am I supposed to measure up to a standard that I don't even know?"

Nana rose and set her hand on Maria's shoulder. "*Chiquita*, your father cares about you very much. He

128

doesn't expect you to be anything other than yourself. It is most likely that whatever he said to you he said out of fear and concern for your well-being."

"Sure he did," Maria said bitterly, turning away, and Nana dropped her hand. After a time, Maria decided to try the subject of her mother again but found she was alone in her room.

Chapter 9

NOVEMBER 1739

"**D**OES IT EVER STOP raining here?" Miguel asked his horse as he navigated the gelding around a cart during a rare break in the weather. "They keep saying it'll dry up soon, but I swear I'm growing moss. How about you?"

The horse ignored his comments and continued on, swatting Miguel with his tail. Miguel sighed. "You've really got to work on your communication skills, my friend. You keep this up, and folk may stop talking to you all together." Miguel snorted. *Not unlike some women I know.*

He looked around, always aware of the people around him, and let his gaze rest on the dark-haired young woman who rode ahead of him. He could always tell when Maria finally noticed him following her. She'd sit up straighter and push her horse to walk faster. Most asinine of all, though, she'd take long circuitous routes to get wherever she meant to travel, as though turning at random. He couldn't bring himself to believe that she meant to lose him; her pace was far too leisurely than that.

Which left the idea that she was just trying to annoy him. It probably would have worked if it hadn't actually made his job easier. The fact that she had no set route made a possible ambush that much more difficult. The fact that her stubborn pride inconvenienced only herself felt like sweet justice.

"At least with the lighter rain, we don't have to play the messenger so much anymore, hey boy?" Miguel asked his gelding, patting it on the neck as Maria turned onto the road that would take her to the Casa de la Cuesta. Now, being sent to carry notes between her and the Señoritas de la Cuesta, that *had* annoyed him. Especially during the heavy rain.

Maria kicked her horse into a trot, and Miguel kept pace until she turned into the drive. He reined in his gelding and watched from the road. He thought he saw her turn back and look at him for just a moment before disappearing into the safety of the great house. Taking a deep breath, he shook his head.

"Come on, boy. We have work to do." Miguel turned the horse and trotted back into the town.

***

"You ought to stop tormenting him." Betania set down her quill and stretched her hands.

"I'm sure I don't know what you're talking about," Maria said, setting a flourish on the fanciful flower she was inking. The invitations for the ball were to go out within the week, and she and Betania had volunteered for the task of writing and embellishing them. A gentle breeze pushed its way through the open windows of the study Maria's father had given her to use.

"Tormenting yourself, then. You perk up every time someone walks by and wilt when it's not him." Betania turned in her chair to give Maria a look.

Maria worked her mouth a moment before she could decide what to say. "I do not. It's just that, well, he's been acting weird."

"You mean aside from being his usually friendly self? Or are you just upset that he's gotten friendly with my sister?"

Maria held back a scowl. "I don't care about Elisa. She throws herself at everyone."

"So why are you avoiding her?" Betania moved the invitation she'd been working on aside and pulled a fresh one toward her, dipping her quill into the ink.

"I'm not avoiding her, she's just so …." Maria made a gagging sound and Betania smiled.

Though, if Maria were honest with herself, she was a little jealous. She missed his companionship. She missed their conversations and the way he smiled when she made him laugh. But now it was Betania's blonde slip of a sister who was speaking to him, when he should have been speaking to her. Elisa always made a point of being friendly with Miguel, and their conversations had become easier and easier. And only the other day, she'd heard Elisa make him laugh.

"Hey, watch it!' Betania exclaimed.

Maria looked down at her paper. She'd pressed too hard, and the red ink had spread across the paper. Maria repressed the urge to crumble up the paper and throw it.

"Sorry, I wasn't paying attention." Maria carefully blotted the ruined page and rose to toss it into the fireplace. She just didn't understand him. She'd been able to avoid him during the heavy rains, but as they'd lightened and she'd had to spend more time outdoors, it seemed Miguel was always around, conveniently busy with another task or just happening to be where she was. He always had something nice to say to her even though she refused to reply. Even worse was when she'd glance at him out of the corner of her eye to find him staring at her, which he did at least half of the time. She returned to her seat beside Betania.

But then he'd go and encourage Elisa's flirting. Maria pulled a fresh sheet toward herself and bit her lip, holding the pen above the ink pot.

Didn't Miguel know she was angry with him? Tapping the ink from the nip, Maria set the pen to paper. She had tried to ignore him, but the harder she tried, the more she caught herself watching him. He never was without his cutlass. She had noticed a pistol butt inside his coat, and he almost never went anywhere without a coat, despite the heat. She also knew that late in the day, a lock of his dark hair would always escape the cord that held the rest of it back, falling directly over one of his eyes.

With a final flourish, she set down the pen and inspected the flower. Finding it satisfactory, she set it aside and reached for the next one. She also knew that he often ran his hand through his hair when it was down, and made motions to do so when it was pulled back. That his green eyes glittered when he laughed but were always dark when he thought himself unseen. That his British accent was stronger when he was tired. That he had a dimple in one cheek when he smiled, which was often. That one of his teeth was somewhat crooked ….

The sound of footsteps along the corridor made her look up and hold her breath, until she realized they were too light to be his. A feeling of disappointment ran through her, and she scowled before shaking it off, turning back to her work.

"If it's not my sister," Betania said, a smile in her voice, "then what is bothering you so much about him?"

"No. I mean, yes, Elisa is bothersome. When is she not? But also, with Miguel. He's friendly and the soul of propriety, but I think my little sea dog is actually following me. It's unnerving."

"You know he doesn't like being called that, right?" Betania said without looking up.

Maria rolled her eyes. "I don't see why it matters if he doesn't like it; it's not like anyone calls him that to his face."

"If you really think he's following you, you should ask him about it," Betania suggested, annoyance creeping into her voice. "If it's that big of a deal to you, you should actually talk about it."

"I would confront him about it," Maria said, shrugging her shoulders as she began again on the invitations, "but as I am not speaking to him until he apologizes for his rude behavior, it will have to wait. I can think of no decent reason that he won't apologize, so I intend to wait."

***

At long last, the day came, late in December, for the invitations to be sent. Having seen the letters on their way, the girls were basked in the rare sunlight in their garden.

"I think this ball is going to be perfectly lovely!" Betania sighed, running her fingers along the spine of a book Maria knew to hold several well-read notes.

"I'm still excited to pick up our masks. They should be ready by tomorrow," Selena said.

"Ours will be the best, of course, since I had the wonderful idea of ordering them made early, before anyone else." Elisa lay back on her bench, far too pleased with her own forethought.

"I'm just glad Miguel isn't invited," Maria said. That very morning he'd had the audacity to tell her good morning with that smile and his beautiful green eyes.

"Whatever do you mean?" Selena asked.

"What do *you* mean?" Maria asked, confused.

"Didn't you know?" Betania gave Maria a cautious look. "Elisa gave him an invitation personally,"

"I see." Maria glared at Elisa.

Elisa sat up straight and attempted to look down her nose at the taller Maria. "I had every right. *You* certainly didn't seem interested in being the one to invite him, so I did. We decided from the start to invite *every* eligible young man, and as I see it, that includes Miguel."

"*He* is nothing but my father's hired hand. We didn't invite any of Selena's body servants."

"What is done is done, Maria. Let it go," Selena cut in.

Maria gave Elisa one last loathing look and walked out of the garden, bidding them a good day over her shoulder.

As Maria stepped through the gate, she looked around expectantly for Miguel. To her surprise and disappointment, he did not appear. When she reached the main house, she ordered her horse brought around, certain he would show up before she left. But when he had still not appeared by the time she mounted up, Maria found herself lingering, hoping he would arrive.

As the light rain had started up again, she sighed and turned her horse toward home. Maria took the long route around the town, wanting to be alone with her thoughts. More than anything, she felt confused. She was angry that Elisa had invited Miguel yet pleased that he would be coming. Angry because Miguel was *her* sea dog to invite or not invite. Pleased when she finally noticed him on his own horse behind her. Angry that he would not actually talk to her but excited when he brought his sable gelding up even with hers. Frustrated

136

that her anticipated night of fun at the ball would be marred by his presence. Thrilled at the prospect that he might ask her to dance.

Maria struggled with her thoughts and the heavy silence between them, acutely aware of both the distance and the closeness of him riding beside her. She dismounted when they reached her home and handed her reins to Antón, the stablehand. She let out a breath, and for a moment, felt that she'd been hit in the gut when Miguel turned his horse and rode back out the gate without a word to her.

That night during supper, Maria, Don Ciro, and Miguel sat in their usual places, when Miguel brought up the subject Maria had hoped to avoid.

"Don Ciro, it appears that I have been invited to a masked ball, to be hosted by the Díaz girls, their cousin, and your daughter," he said, his voice a model of cordiality.

"Is that so?" Ciro looked at his daughter. "Maria, you never told me you'd been planning a masque."

An uncomfortable feeling of being trapped began in the pit of her stomach. "Doña Olivia advised that we not tell anyone until the invitations had been sent."

"A wise decision from a wise woman. As I am sure she has been overseeing the plans, I have no objection to your going, Maria." Ciro nodded.

"What about Miguel, Papa?" Maria's heart sank even as she asked. She knew what he'd say.

Ciro looked long and hard at Miguel before answering. "As long as he attends to all of his duties that day, I would consider it a slight to my hospitality if he did not attend."

"With all due respect, Don Ciro, I will only go with Maria's permission," Miguel said quietly.

Don Ciro raised an eyebrow at him. "What do you mean her permission? Didn't you just say she invited you?"

"No, Señor. It was the younger Señorita de la Cuesta who gave me the invitation, and without your daughter's knowledge. Seeing as your daughter holds some grudge against me, it would be dishonorable to go to her own ball against her wishes." Miguel caught Maria's gaze and held it for the first time in weeks.

Maria felt as though all the air had been sucked from the room.

Don Ciro looked at his daughter as well, raising an expectant eyebrow.

Maria took a breath and centered herself to speak as coolly as she could manage. "I care for Elisa as a sister, and if she wishes for Miguel to be there, I shall not stand in the way."

"Maria," Don Ciro warned.

"Oh, fine." Maria sighed. *I'll do it for you, Papa.* She turned to address Miguel directly. "Miguel, I would be honored if you attended our ball."

"Of course, m'lady." Miguel stood and bowed while Ciro flashed an impish grin.

"I'm afraid I have a headache and must retire for the night." Maria scowled at them. Clearly, she had lost. "Good evening."

138

The men stood as she did, and she stalked toward the main house, heading straight for her bedroom.

***

"You know, Miguel," Ciro said, looking after his daughter as she glided from the room, "I don't believe she knows how graceful she really is."

"No, Señor, I don't believe she does," Miguel said. *Or how amazingly beautiful she is, either,* he thought, staring after her long after she was gone, letting his food grow cold.

Chapter 10

T HREE WEEKS before the ball, and with some prodding from Nana, Maria decided to officially break the silence with Miguel. It would be in her best interest, after all. She refused to cede the point that she was being rude and childish, but she was willing to accept that the ball would be far more pleasant if she could be cordial with everyone. And that included Miguel. Not to mention, of course, that she might cause gossip and tarnish her father's reputation if she appeared snobbish. Hurting her father intentionally was one thing Maria simply could not do.

Maria paced the hall before her room, steeling her nerves. *Nana is going to come down that hall any moment and chide you for wearing a hole in the carpet,* Maria scolded herself. *All right, just go for it.* Taking a deep breath, she turned to the stairs and descended for breakfast.

The walk from the staircase to the dining room seemed to last for miles, especially once she glimpsed Miguel from the covered walkway. She paused just outside the door and rolled her shoulders, holding her head high before entering.

"*Buenos días,* Señorita Álvarez," Miguel greeted her as he usually did.

"*Buenos días,* Miguel," Maria said briskly, nodding in his direction.

Miguel's double-take and look of caution nearly undid her as she rounded the table. It was all she could do to keep from laughing. Why hadn't she done this sooner? She leaned across the table to snag the first fruit she happened to touch. She hastened from the room and smirked at the sound his chair scraping across the floor, as Miguel stood for her a moment too late.

Maria practically ran back to her room, shutting the door behind her. Had he come out and watched her flight? She leaned against the door, trying to catch her breath and calm the giddiness that filled her. She set the fruit on her table, actually noticing it for the first time. *Mango. Great.* They had eaten mangoes together the first morning Miguel had stayed in her father's house. How long ago had that been? Maria could hardly remember a time when Miguel had not been in her life. Almost a year, perhaps.

That was right; it was just after Alistair had died. They'd met the next morning. Maria felt a sudden pang of guilt as she realized that, aside from the occasional dreams of him beside her, she hadn't thought about her dog in months. Not since her head had been so filled with Miguel. A flare of anger rose in her chest, but she smothered it before it could catch. She was nearly seventeen, a woman grown. It was time to start behaving like one, as her father had told her. His cutting remarks from that night still stung, making her vision blur with tears. Those she pushed back down, too. She was a woman now, and she would make her father proud.

Maria moved to her wash-basin and splashed water on her face. She would show Miguel that she was not to be trifled with any longer. She fixed her hair and changed into one of her nicest dresses with Nana's help. As she settled the last of her outfit together, Maria looked in the mirror, pleased with what she saw. She stood up straighter, throwing back her shoulders and holding her head high. She would show him.

As she left the room, she saw Nana shaking her head and smiling to herself. Maria almost paused to ask why but decided she didn't want to know.

For the rest of that day, Maria continued to reply to Miguel if he spoke to her first, but always briskly and briefly. To her dismay, she found she could not manage the easy banter they had enjoyed before. Over the next few days, she applied herself to responding more warmly and engaging him in conversation. At first, his responses were terse, but soon they were speaking amicably again. She even found herself laughing at his jokes from time to time, though she could not yet get him to laugh.

Oddly though, Maria noticed he would only speak with her openly when nobody of consequence was around. Whenever anyone from either her household or the Casa de la Cuesta appeared, he would clam up and return to his previous brusque manner.

And then there was Elisa. Somehow, he remained friendly with Elisa.

Each time she saw so much as a look pass between them, Feelings rolled over her so strongly they threatened to drown her. Anger, jealousy, dark feelings she had no name for, but she pushed them down, forced them away, stood up taller, and focused on smiling.

Then, when Maria and Miguel would walk together, and he would take her arm or speak her name or even look at her, she would be filled with even more confusing feelings. Feelings that made her feel as though she would burst with joy, as well as yet more ebullient feelings that she could not name but wanted to bask in. Those too, she shoved down, though she did not try to rid herself of them completely.

***

Miguel found that he did not trust Maria's quicksilver emotions. They reminded him too much of being at sea with the air heavy before a storm, unsure if or when the torrent would begin. In his time with the Álvarez family, he had come to enjoy their sense of stability, even if it was like a sturdy ship in shark-infested waters. Rolling his shoulders, he flexed the stiff material of the shockingly high quality great coat she had presented him with two days before. He wouldn't be surprised to see this coat last for years. The subtle blue-grey cloth fit him perfectly from the cut to the lack of ornate embellishment.

"Gonza still insisting that you lost his merchandise?" Dom, the Álvarez steward, asked Don Ciro as they inspected his ship, the gulls overhead crying out with their usual noise.

Miguel stood before the large hatch, eyeing the workers hauling the cargo ashore. Now that Maria was speaking to him again, the days seemed brighter, but he hated to trust to hope. *I'm just her father's hired man,* he reminded himself, as he did several times a day. Yet the way she'd smile at him, her face lighting up when she noticed him, would make his heart skip a beat or his feet miss a step. And then there was the great coat, a deep blue-grey with silvered buttons and pockets deep enough to keep a pistol in; without a doubt the finest gift he'd ever received. But then Doña Olivia's warning would creep back into his head. These girls—Maria— were not for the likes of him. No matter how she smiled at him.

"No, much worse." Don Ciro began his descent into the hold. "He is claiming I stole it."

Dom followed Don Ciro below as the smells of the ship—wood, tar, and the acrid smells of humans living too close together for too long—swirled around Miguel. They pulled at him, and he wrinkled his nose. His father's ship—Miguel shook his head. Convinced that the supercargo had the workers well in hand and none planned to drop their crate and attack them, Miguel followed the men into the hold.

144

It wasn't a matter of being too cautious, either. That very thing had actually happened the first time Don Ciro had brought Miguel on an inspection. Miguel hadn't taken the possibility of danger quite as seriously then. He had supposed that tempers couldn't run as high on land, with all the space and freedom that came with it.

With a tight smile, Miguel shook his head at his naivety as he moved through the dark, dank hold toward the other men. With a hand set cautiously on his belt knife, he watched the gloomy corners but saw no one. What he really needed was to put Maria out of his mind.

"Will he accept payment for the missing goods?" Dom asked as they moved through the hold.

"Would that even be a good idea?" Miguel asked as he reached them. Don Ciro raised an eyebrow. "I mean, if he is lying about it and you paid him, essentially rewarding his dishonesty, wouldn't he just do it again?"

"Even if he's not lying and his merchandise never made it to him, if I paid him for it, he might try this again," Don Ciro said with a nod, shifting a crate to the side. "He's pulled this before, but I have been able to prove that his goods were delivered, and he has dropped the matter. But this time is different. I am certain the goods made it ashore. The manifest says they were unloaded, but they disappeared from the warehouse."

"Couldn't you report it as a theft?" Miguel suggested, making his way down a row of empty hammocks that swung gently with the rocking of the ship.

"If anything else was missing, he could," Dom said. "Everyone knows of their rivalry, so if this comes to light it will serve only to hurt Ciro."

"Which is, of course, always the goal." Miguel nodded. "So why hasn't he done something like this sooner?"

Ciro crouched down and hefted a barrel onto his shoulder, then turned back toward the hatch. "Because this time he wants something from me, and I refuse to give it."

Miguel gave Dom a sideways look as their employer walked past them, a determined look on his face.

Dom shook his head. "If he wants you to know, he'll tell you."

Miguel moved to follow Dom out of the hold. Whatever it was Gonza wanted, if Don Ciro had refused to give it to him so far, Miguel could be sure he wasn't going to. But how far Gonza would go to obtain this mysterious thing? And would it put Maria in danger?

As he clambered out of the ship, Miguel grimaced at the bright sunlight, half expecting to be clubbed on the head. But Dom and Don Ciro were before him, their stances relaxed, and no shadows moved behind him. Giving a discreet assessment of the deck, Miguel took his place beside the older men, who were now speaking with the captain.

The salty, fishy air filled his nose. He sighed internally. There was just no getting around it. He cared for Maria, too much perhaps. But did she actually care for him back, or was she like the ocean? He eyed the clouds in the distance. Fickle, temperamental, seeing him as just another plaything to use and discard at her whim. A part of him rebelled at the thought, loyally declaring that she had so much more substance to her than that. *And yet she didn't speak to me for weeks because she felt slighted.* He had no response for that. The distant ringing of the church bells brought Miguel back to himself.

"It is time for me to be on my way, señors," Miguel cut in with a bow. Don Ciro gave a wave of dismissal, and with a curt nod, Miguel turned from them, the length of his great coat flaring behind him. Time. An unwelcome flickering of hope flared up in his chest. He would give her time, and perhaps she would see him as more.

Chapter 11

M ARIA WOKE early the day of the ball, getting up even before the sun had risen. Neither her lingering dream of Alistair growling beside her nor her ever-more-confusing feelings towards Miguel could dampen her excitement as she prepared for the ball.

She and Nana spent part of the day deciding how to arrange some of the ribbons they had purchased in the days prior. Early afternoon found Maria preparing her long black hair and getting her into her dark red gown. As she and Nana were applying the finishing touches, there was a knock on the door.

"Come in," Maria called, watching the door through her mirror.

"We're nearly finished," Nana called out at the same time.

Maria watched as the door opened and her father stepped into the room. She smiled and stood, rushing over to give him a hug. He hugged her back and then, after a moment, pulled her away and stared down into her face.

"My word, Maria. Is that really you?" Ciro asked. Maria blushed and looked away. "Nana, I think I have seen a vision. Come over here and see if you see it, too."

"Oh, I can see it quite well from here, Señor. I have watched her transform before my very eyes these past few months," Nana said.

"Tell me, Papa—" Maria stepped back a few steps and smiled up at her father "—what is this vision that you and Nana are sharing?"

But Ciro just stood where he was, shaking his head slowly. Maria gave Nana a questioning look.

"Why, you are appearing as a profound likeness of your mother." Nana gave Maria a smile. "Much like she did when they first met, I might add."

"Do I really, Papa?" Maria's heart filled with pride. After all this time, had she finally done justice to her mother's memory? "Do you think mother would be proud?"

"Absolutely, *mi querida*. I think your mother would be very proud of you, and I know that I am." Ciro's voice was full of emotion as he pulled a box from his pocket. "Here, I have something for you. I would be pleased if you would wear it tonight."

"What is it?" Maria asked as her father opened the box.

"It was your mother's, something her mother had given to her, and her mother before that. I had it refitted to something more in today's style." Ciro opened the box and unwrapped the fold of silk cloth. Maria gasped as a necklace she had never seen before was revealed.

"It's beautiful!" she breathed, reaching for it to take a closer look.

Gently, her father laid it in her hand. The necklace was a choker of pearls with ribbons on the end to tie it. In the center of the pearls hung a worked silver pendant, nearly as long as her thumb, triangular, and holding a carved red stone. Around the stone, the silver was set with a dozen tiny diamonds. Ciro lifted it by the strand of pearls, and the red stone, hung independently within the silver setting, rotated as though to show off its color. Maria tore her gaze from the necklace and looked back at her father with a bright smile.

"When I first met your mother, she wore the stone in a beaded setting that she had made herself as a young woman. When I was preparing to … ask for her hand, I arranged for her to 'lose' it one day." Ciro laughed as he handed the box to Nana and moved to place the necklace on Maria's throat. "Actually, I had her brother steal it from her."

"It was a naughty thing you did, too," Nana chided him as she removed the matching pearl and jasper earrings and fastened them in Maria's ears. Then, addressing Maria, she continued. "Ayelen was so distraught over its loss that she did not eat for three days and did not smile for a week. I'm not sure she would ever have forgiven either her brother *or* your father for putting her through that anxiety."

150

"What happened then?" Maria asked her father, devouring every little tidbit she could get about her mother.

"Well, I had it set into some metalwork, nothing as nice as it is now, as I was not so well off then, and returned it to her when I asked her to marry me."

"How romantic!" Maria exclaimed.

"Not really." Ciro grinned ruefully as Nana guffawed.

"Ayelen was so angry, she thought he had stolen it," Nana said. "That was bad enough, you see, but then she thought he was trying to pa—"

"Trying to give her something that was already hers," Ciro cut Nana off with a dark look.

"What did she do?" Maria touched the necklace as she looked into the mirror, wondering just how much of her reflection was her mother looking back at her.

"Well, she pulled the stone out of the setting and tried to throw the rest of it into the river." Ciro said with a shrug. "I stopped her, and once I had calmed her down and explained the situation, she relented."

Maria wondered what she had said that had drained the mirth from his eyes.

"He neglects to mention that she slapped him and 'calming her down,' 'explaining the situation' and her 'relenting' took a good two weeks," Nana whispered into Maria's ear, and Maria giggled.

"She did let me replace the setting, though. And she rarely took it off until you were born, *mi querida*. Before she died, she told me that I was to give it to you when you … 'decided to become a woman' were the words she used." Ciro smiled at her. "So, you see, I think she would be very proud of you. As, indeed, am I."

A knock on the door announced that the coach was ready, and Ciro offered his daughter his arm. Maria took it, and he led her out the door. She could hardly contain her joy. Her father had finally forgiven her for her poor attitude, and *perhaps* she could admit it had been childish. Her mother's necklace lay cool and comforting against her skin.

As they reached the stairs, Maria saw Miguel standing at the bottom waiting for them, still wearing his cutlass, though now it was in a beautiful scabbard. He looked up at them and smiled, and warmth filled her. She smiled and looked away from him as Ciro gave her a nudge toward the stairs. She looked back at him for a moment before descending, wishing she could tell him how grateful she felt. When she reached the bottom Miguel held out his hand. She hesitated a moment before laying her bare hand in his. It was the first time they'd touched in two months, and a thrill shot up her arm at the contact.

Miguel led her to the waiting coach, and Maria nodded up to Diego, the driver, who gave her a discreet wink. Grinning, Maria let Miguel help up into the coach, and as she settled her skirts about her, Ciro touched Miguel's shoulder.

"Take care of her, Miguel," he said gravely.

"I will, Señor," Miguel nodded to him and took a seat across from Maria.

Ciro turned to his daughter, one hand on the coach door. "I love you, Maria. Never forget that."

"I love you, too, Papa," Maria returned, surprised at the unusual display of sentiment.

Her father shut the door and stepped away.

Maria couldn't think of anything to say as the coach started forward. What a strange exchange. Though she had never doubted his affection, her father rarely told her he loved her, and never in public like that before. And what had that been with Miguel? What was going on?

Unwilling to let the puzzle ruin her evening, she decided to save it for later and distracted herself by studying Miguel's outfit. He wore an embroidered coat, but nothing on it announced him as having any affiliation with the Álvarez house. He wore gloves and polished knee-high boots, but she could see they were well worn and likely far more comfortable than her own shoes.

In fact, now that she looked closely, she could see that everything he was wearing spoke of much use and comfort to the wearer, though well cleaned and fitting enough for the ball. When had he found time to break in such fancy clothes? It didn't surprise her, though. He was her father's man, and he looked every bit the part. She wondered what other weaponry besides his cutlass he had stashed away on his person this time, and where he would be keeping it. Perhaps next to his skin, the metal warming from the heat of his body ....

Blushing, she looked away. When she dared to look back, she saw that he was studying her, too, and she quickly looked down at her own hands.

"What do you see?" she asked him, picking up her mask and fiddling with it.

"I see ... a vision of beauty. You shall be the envy of the night, I am sure," Miguel said. "Actually, I believe I am mistaken. *I* shall be the envy of the ball tonight."

"What do you mean?" Maria looked up at him.

"I mean that every young man who sees you shall envy me for being by your side, wishing that they were in my place."

"I see," said Maria skeptically.

"What do you see?" Miguel leaned back, draping his arm across the seat back.

"I see a young man who can't seem to go anywhere without his sword. Honestly, do you really expect to get into a fight tonight? I've only ever seen you draw it once. I'd almost believe that you've no idea how to use the thing," she said, trying to sound playful.

"Do you now? Tell me, what else do you *almost* believe?"

"I don't really know, Miguel." Maria sighed. *I believe I missed you. I believe you infuriate me.* "I've been so confused about, well, everything since you came around. I can't seem to figure you out one way or the other. You don't use your real name, you don't tell

154

anyone the truth about yourself, and you're always following me despite constant work for my father, and yet for some reason he trusts you explicitly. Who knows what to believe about you?"

"I am a mystery. I know no more truth than you do." Miguel smiled and raised his mask to his face. "Tell me what you want to believe about me, and tonight I will be it for you."

I want to believe ... But she wouldn't allow herself to think it even as her eyes traced the contours and lines of his mask, avoiding contact with the green eyes behind it. "I don't want to make things up about you."

"What do you want then?" Miguel asked as she finally met his eyes.

Her heart sped up. "What any woman wants, I suppose." Maria shrugged and looked away, only to find her gaze drawn back to his, as inevitable as a flower turning toward the sun.

Miguel raised an eyebrow and leaned forward. "Enlighten me."

"I don't know." Maria's mind was muddled; she could hardly think with him looking at her like that. And his voice ... She took a deep breath and tried to set her feelings to words. "A man I can trust not to leave me, who will take care of me. Someone reliable and dependable, everything my father is and more. Someone who won't just leave at the next tide. Who is not ... I don't know ...." Maria ran out of words and gestured helplessly.

"You mean, not a sailor?" Miguel sat back, lowering his mask.

"I didn't mean that," Maria backpedaled, confused by the change in his voice.

"But you did. You do. Am I really just another sea dog to you? A pet, biddable and amusing, then ultimately disposable? Tell me Maria, if I left, how long would you mourn me? The dog got a few days; do you think I would merit a week?"

"Miguel, really, I didn't mean to say—"

"But you did say it. But it is nice to know what you think of me, and what I can never be to you." Miguel forced his voice back to lightness, but the chill in it struck Maria through the heart. "It frees me to move on. There are so many other lovely ladies in Maracaibo, especially the younger Señorita de la Cuesta."

The coach stopped abruptly. They had arrived. Tears pushed up behind Maria's eyes, and she raised her mask to cover the struggle to force them back down. She would be strong, like her mother.

"If all you are is another sea dog, I hope you will at least have the decency to escort me in before you go chasing off after the next bit of driftwood in the surf," Maria said coldly.

Miguel helped her out, and, without giving him another moment's concern, she threw her shoulders back and walked as regally as she could into the house. She could feel him walking silently beside her, half a step behind. A pang went through her that he had not taken her arm as they walked in, but she swallowed it down. She didn't want him to, anyhow.

True to Miguel's prediction, every eye turned toward her as she walked through the crowd. After a few minutes, when the first young man came and asked her to dance, she realized that Miguel had slipped off. She accepted cordially and set herself to enjoying the evening.

The decorations were stunning and everyone was in the most beautiful gowns she had ever seen. She had never been to any party in Maracaibo with such elegance and vibrancy, the latter of which she attributed to the age of the crowd. Maria spent most of the evening dancing with the young men. At one point, she picked out Betania from the crowd, dancing with Benito Garcia, the young man Betania had insisted be invited. Maria did not see one without the other nearby for the rest of the evening.

After one especially lively dance, Maria decided that she'd had enough fun for the moment and begged her partner for some air. She sent him off for a drink and made her way to the balcony which stretched the length of the ballroom, enjoying the feel of the cool night air. Leaning against the banister, she looked over the dark plantation to the jungles beyond. Maria fancied she could almost hear the call of the wild birds and animals through the sounds of merrymaking inside. Her sight wandered up into the velvety sky and the stars that glittered across it. The moon had not risen yet, and the "great river of stars," as Nana had always called them, shone bright and clear.

The music began again, and Maria wondered idly where her previous dance partner had gone off to. Voices out on the lawn below the balcony drew Maria's gaze back down to earth. She smiled. Some day she might walk down a garden path in the moonlight with the man she loved. Whoever that was.

Shifting her weight sent an ache through her feet. Maria was not yet ready to return to the lights and sounds of the party. Instead, she moved to a more secluded part of the balcony and sat on a bench, enjoying the feel of the cool, smooth stone beneath her fingers. The mountains to the northwest stood in silhouette beneath the night sky, and Maria wondered, not for the first time, what was beyond them. She'd continued to have regular dreams of Alistair, but each time she drew closer to the jungle that lay at the mountain's feet, covering them like a rich green blanket. And each time her dog grew more agitated with her as she gazed at them. Maria gave a half smile. She could almost hear him now, like an echo of music in a large hall, growling his warning beneath the music.

The music inside stopped, and Maria shook herself from her reverie. It was probably time she returned. She wasn't even certain how long she'd been out here. Hadn't anyone noticed she was gone? Miguel, at least—but no. Her face fell. Taking a deep breath, she stood and moved toward the door. Just then, Elisa came out, pulling a young man out onto the balcony. That it

158

was Elisa was obvious, despite her mask; no one else could bounce as much as that girl. Curious to know who she had ensnared, Maria stepped back into the shadows and watched.

Elisa pulled the young man up to the balcony banister and leaned out over it, breaking off a spray of lavender and holding it up to her nose. The young man stood placidly beside her, speaking in quiet tones. There was something familiar about him, something that made Maria uncomfortable, but the shadows obscured them. Elisa reached up and threw her arms around the man, leaning against him. Maria held back a snort, she could imagine Doña Olivia's reaction if she heard of Elisa behaving in such a way. The young man pulled her arms down from around his neck, leading her around a nearby pillar. A tightness filled Maria's stomach. She shouldn't be spying on them. He swung Elisa around, setting her back against the pillar and, with one hand on the stone beside her head and the other holding both her hands at her chest, he leaned in and spoke in her ear.

Embarrassed, Maria looked away. It was time to make a discreet exit. She tried not to look at the couple as she passed, but her need to satisfy her curiosity about the young man's identity overruling her sense of propriety, and she glanced up.

Maria found herself staring straight into Miguel's eyes. He'd chosen that moment to look up, and it stopped her cold. Maria's breathing stopped. Sound stopped. Time stopped. Maria was trapped in Miguel's beautiful green eyes.

Her eyes slid over to Elisa with her petulant smile. Something broke inside Maria, and, like strings snapped on a marionette, her whole body sagged. She didn't register Miguel's pained look as he pushed Elisa away from him. She turned and walked blindly back into the house.

She'd made it halfway across the ballroom when Miguel caught up to her.

"Maria, please," Miguel pleaded, his voice barely loud enough to be heard over the music.

"Go away, Miguel," Maria said in a pained whisper.

"That wasn't what it looked like." He tried to grab Maria's arm and make her face him, but she jerked free.

"Please, leave me alone." Maria could hardly hear her own voice as she continued her swift pace to the door.

"Maria ...." Miguel followed her into the hall.

She turned abruptly and faced him. "You're always following me, Miguel. Always watching, always nearby. Why are you spying on me?" she hissed at him.

Miguel just stood there, at a loss for an answer.

"Heh. That's what I thought. Just leave me alone, Miguel. I've had nothing but trouble since you showed up. For once in your meddlesome life here, leave me alone!" She shoved him back into the ballroom. He stumbled a little, caught himself and stood there, watching as all his hopes and dreams he'd been too afraid to accept until that very moment disappeared down the hall with the dark-haired girl in the red dress.

160

***

Elisa watched the interchange from across the room and sneered as Maria walked off by herself. She felt a twist of anger inside her, a bitterness she'd felt before but never to the extent of maliciousness. Without a care toward how her actions would change the course of her life, she sought out one of the head servants and ordered that for the remainder of the night, Maria was not to be disturbed, not to be approached, and not to be watched. Then, to soothe her hurt pride, she resumed throwing herself at the young men.

Chapter 12

M ARIA PASSED through the halls of the plantation home without noticing or caring where she went, blind to all around her. She had practically grown up in the Casa de la Cuesta and had no fear of losing her way. An unseasonably chill breeze bit at her bare arms, bringing her to the realization that she'd gone outside. She rubbed her hands over her arms, willing the goosebumps to relax. She looked down at her bare hands with chagrin, wishing she'd brought gloves. Unwilling to go back inside, she started across the lawn. The shadows beside her moved, startling her.

"Señorita Álvarez," someone called to her in a hushed whisper.

"Yes?" she asked cautiously.

The man motioned to her closer, as if afraid of being seen. "Señorita, I have long been in the employ of your father, Don Álvarez. In fact, I've known him since long before he settled down here in Maracaibo. He is a good and honorable man."

Maria noted that the man, a mestizo by the look of him, wore de la Cuesta livery. He likely lived in the western part of the town, the "Maracaibo mestiza," which was composed of the lowest social group. It was neither surprising nor uncommon that one should be among the servants here, but it did seem unlikely that any had sailed with her father. Unlikely, too, that such a one, who seemed so devoted to him, would have willingly chosen this place rather than the service of her father.

With these doubts in her mind, she guardedly came closer. "I am aware of the qualities of my father. But who are you, and why do you wish to remain unnoticed?"

"Punishment is severe for those who disobey orders in the de la Cuesta plantation, but worse is the wrath of your father, whose man I remain."

Maria's stomach constricted with apprehension. "What orders? What are you talking about?"

"We have been ordered to not attend you in any way for the remainder of the evening. However, there are many who have been placed here for your safety. Over the years, most have forgotten their debts to Señor Álvarez, but I have not. I cannot protect you outright; that is his job, but I feel I must at least warn you."

"Warn me of what?" Maria was not sure what to think.

"Señorita, your father has many enemies. Many very powerful enemies, who will hurt him any way they can. And that includes you. It is not as safe here as it once was, and tonight everyone in Maracaibo knows you are here. And now we have been ordered to turn our backs to you, and no one here will dare to disobey such a direct command, coming from so high." They heard voices drawing near, and he backed away, looking frightened.

"What is going on?" she hissed at him.

"I have said too much already. Go back inside, and do not let yourself be caught alone tonight." And with that, the strange mestizo disappeared back into the shadows.

Maria stared after him in wonder, feeling her world shaken to its foundations. After a moment she shook her head, trying to dispel her trepidation. Enemies. Right. Her father had been a captain for the East India Company before she was born. It had been an honorable business venture, and he had settled here to raise her after making his fortune. He'd built a business and partnered with Dons Sergio Díaz, Elisa and Betania's father, and Vasco Abano, Selena's father. His business here was as reputable as he was. How could he have enemies? Surely there might be people out there who didn't like him, but in seventeen years he'd had no trouble that she knew of. Why should there be any tonight?

With these consoling thoughts Maria shook her head one more time at the crazy servant and turned back toward the gardens as a light breeze toyed with her hair. Despite her reassurances, a chill ran down her spine as she noticed for the first time the many deep shadows. Gardens that had seemed so peaceful and romantic just a short time before now made her hesitate. Chiding herself for being silly, Maria turned back toward the house. Silly or not, she was determined to do more to be the responsible young woman her father expected her to be.

The gaiety of the party still felt abrasive, however, so she turned to walk around the north wing of the house and return through the front doors. Surely there would be plenty of light and people between here and there. Walking the perimeter of the large house would give her time to recuperate from the emotional trauma Miguel had inflicted before returning to the ball.

Miguel. Really, he was the source of all her problems. She'd been so happy until he came around. Why did he follow her around all the time, anyway? Perhaps it was because he liked her, maybe wanting to court her. She pursed her lips. He was far too outgoing for such subtlety. Perhaps he really was interested in Elisa. Again, her heart fell as she remembered him leaning in toward her, whispering in her ear. What was he saying? Had they kissed when she wasn't looking?

She clenched her fists. *I don't care what he was saying or if he kissed her!* she shouted in her mind. *If he wants some other girl, he should have her. I care too much for him to hold him back.* The thought stopped her in her tracks. *I care too much for him? Do I really care for him that much?*

She began forward again, aware that she was in shadow, but the burning question of just how much did she care for Miguel consumed her attention. A part of her wanted to admit that she loved him, perhaps even was in love with him. All the rest of her refused the thought; all her pride and anger and frustration, fought the idea of loving him. He was the reason for all her problems. But she did care for him.

Struggling with her feelings, she slowed to a stop, her focus too inward to notice the world around her. Movement caught her eye, snapping her from her reverie. A large man in ill-fitting clothing swaggered toward her. Worried, but trying to keep her head about her, she angled to the side, away from the house. The man smiled and mirrored her movements.

She turned abruptly to go back the way she'd come. Three more men flanked her, walking toward her with the same arrogant stride and hard looks. The crazy mestizo's warning resounded in her mind, and, without thinking, she bolted between them. The idea that they would be expecting her to run never passed through Maria's mind.

They caught her with ease.

Before she knew what was happening, cloth was stuffed in her mouth, her arms were behind her back, and she was on her knees. Why was this happening to her? Her racing heartbeat sounded in her ears as she looked around, hoping to see someone in the shadows. Anyone. But there was nothing. This couldn't be real.

"'Ello there, dearie," the man said with a heavy English accent. He knelt in front of her and lifted her chin. The stink of his unwashed body made her recoil.

"Wot a pretty thing you are," another man sneered. Reality crashed into her, and she began to struggle to free her arms as she tried not to panic.

"Lucky for you our master wants you in one piece. And undamaged, if possible," the kneeling man said.

"Now, 'ere's the deal. See this 'ere knife?" He pulled a long, curved knife from somewhere unseen and held it before her face.

She froze, her guts like ice, and nodded.

"Now, tha's a lovely dress yer wearing, dearie, and probably quite costly. Am I right?" Maria nodded again as the world around her seemed to narrow to the knife and the hand that held it.

"I wouldna want to damage such a lovely dress. I'm going to hold this knife to yer ribs, and we are going to walk to the front and git inter yer carriage as though there ain't nothing in the world wrong. Are you following me so far?"

Maria nodded. A stray thought, wondering if the knife would be sharp enough to cut the cloth cleanly or tear it ragged, pushed to the fore of her mind.

Knife Man leaned a little closer. "Now, we'll take this thing out of yer mouth on the condition that you not make a sound, and we'll leave yer ... dress ... undamaged as long as you do what we say, without arousing suspicion. Are we clear?"

Maria nodded once again, her throat so tight that she couldn't have spoken if she'd tried.

"We've already taken the liberty to 'order' yer coach. It will be waiting right over there." Knife Man jerked his head toward the front.

"Stand 'er up!' he hissed. The man behind her jerked on her arms, forcing her painfully to her feet, and she stumbled, unable to feel the ground beneath her. He snickered, twisting her arms further.

Knife Man nodded and grinned, coming up close behind and placing the tip of his knife in the center of her back. The pressure of it through her corset made her want to giggle at the absurdity of it all.

Don't panic! Maria took a deep breath through her nose, determined to calm herself enough to think straight.

"Good. Now let's go, darlin'."

Her arms were released, and she fumbled with numb fingers to pull the gag from her mouth. She crumbled it into her fist to keep from shaking. With another steadying breath, she held her head high and clenched her trembling jaw. She had too much pride to let them see her weakness, and strode forward. Certainly someone would notice the odd group. The pounding in her ears decreased as she walked. Any moment now, someone would stop them.

They rounded the corner, and her carriage stood before them. Her knees almost buckled, first with relief, then fear as she realized the driver, though wearing the Álvarez livery, was not one of her father's men. Nausea filled her stomach. *What had they had done with Diego?* She'd known him since she was a child; surely he'd be all right. He'd find her father and let him know. But what if he wasn't? What if they'd hurt him? Diego would never have let them take the coach without a fight. Panic pushed up against her throat, and she cut off that line of thought. She needed to keep her head.

168

Maria took a hesitant step forward and looked toward the building. People milled around the front entrance of the Casa de la Cuesta. Could she scream? Run across the courtyard to them and safety? The knife suddenly lay on the side of her neck, unnaturally cold.

"Keep movin'."

With one last longing look at the warmly lit entrance, she walked to the waiting carriage. One of the men shoved her through the carriage door, and she stumbled in, falling to her knees. Quickly, she gathered her skirts and threw herself into the corner as Knife Man and another man climbed in, sitting across from her. The other two climbed aboard outside, and the horses started forward. Maria wrapped her arms around herself, determined to hold herself together, even as the trembling in her stomach increased.

The faint music from the house followed them down the drive, and Maria felt the Casa de la Cuesta had never looked so beautiful as it did just then, just out of reach.

Her heart sank as she realized she was on her own. No one was coming for her. No one even knew she was gone.

Chapter 13

MIGUEL PACED the hall just outside the ballroom of the Casa de la Cuesta. How had things turned out so wrong? He had been such an idiot to allow Elisa to get him alone. The end of the hall came too quickly, and he did an abrupt about-face and stalked back the way he'd come. But how was he supposed to have known that Maria would see?

You shouldn't have been so quick to lose your temper with her, Mick. Miguel pulled on his cutlass, lifting it half an inch from the scabbard and shoving it back down as he walked. No, he shouldn't have let himself get attached. He was just a hired hand, nothing more. Just another stray dog to be given table scraps until he was no longer amusing, and then thrown out with the trash. Why should this place have been any different?

He stopped abruptly at the other end of the hall before an ornate table with a large mirror hung above it. *Don Ciro has never treated you that way. He trusted you with his daughter's safety.* Miguel scowled at his reflection. As she'd so brutally told him, she didn't need him being her nanny. She was safe here. He turned from the mirror and strode back down the hall. So why did he feel so anxious?

Miguel knew all of Álvarez's men at the Casa de la Cuesta. Had Don Ciro felt they were insufficient or untrustworthy, he would have told Miguel. Miguel's step faltered. Hadn't Don Ciro given just such directions when they'd left? Miguel stepped into the doorway and scanned the crowd in the ballroom, hoping to see her. He cursed himself for a fool at having let her go off alone.

"Where could you be?" he muttered under his breath. Could she have gone to the gardens? He changed course for the rear of the house. Or perhaps she'd decided to go home. He paused. He could check with the stables. But what if she came back while he was gone? Scowling again, he resumed his determined stride toward the end of the hall.

A man in de la Cuesta livery entered the hall and brushed against Miguel's shoulder. Alarmed, Miguel followed the servant into the ballroom. The man relieved the nearest servant of their drink tray, circled around, and brought it to Miguel with a bow.

"Señorita Álvarez is in trouble. She is alone outside, and I fear for her safety," he murmured, for Miguel's ears only. "We have been ordered to stay away from her."

Miguel waved away the drink, and the serving man wandered back into the crowd. *You miserable, worthless cur,* he berated himself, turning on his heel to exit the room. *You can't even follow simple instructions.*

Over the previous year, Miguel had made a point of becoming familiar with the ins and outs of the entire de la Cuesta plantation. Putting his knowledge to use, he ducked through halls and into the kitchen. Then he was outside, the moonlit darkness pulling him up short at its emptiness. *Let her be safe,* he prayed to anyone who would listen as he ran to the rear of the house. Several couples lingered on the balconies, but fear twisted his gut as he realized none of them were the dark-haired girl in the red dress. He turned and ran back to the stable yard, his eyes searching frantically for the Álvarez coach.

A moment of hope dared to flare inside him when he found the space for the Álvarez coach empty. She had gone home then. As he neared, movement in the darkness urged him forward. Diego, Ciro's driver, lay on the ground, clutching his head. Miguel bolted for the common room in the stables where the hands would be enjoying their own get-together. Why had he wasted so much time? He stopped in the doorway, located another of Don Ciro's men, and nodded him outside.

"Maria has been taken. I believe she is in your master's coach. Get me two fast horses saddled quickly. The driver is in the stall; he is alive, but bleeding. You ride as fast as you can and get more men from Don Ciro. I will go after Maria."

The stable hand gave a smart nod and rushed to a different part of the stable, rousing two stableboys to assist. Miguel held himself back from simply running out into the night after her, but the waiting galled him. The moment the stable hand turned the saddled horse from the stall, Miguel took the reins, swung up onto the gelding's back, and kicked him into a gallop, lying against the horse's neck as they bolted through the door. The hoofbeats of the stable hand's mount sounded behind him on the hard-packed dirt road.

Soon they parted ways, the stablehand veering toward the docks. Miguel turned his horse down the dark road that led around the town. He was taking a chance that they would have preferred to avoid eyes that might recognize something amiss. After all, that was what he would have done. He urged his horse faster down the moonlit road.

***

The curtains in the coach had been drawn closed and Knife Man had put away his knife. Maria's mind raced at the possibilities. Perhaps she could attack him and get the knife away. But no, he was far too strong for her. Could she lunge for the door and throw herself out? As though in response to the idea, the coach abruptly picked up speed. Maria's heart raced at the increase in the horses' pace, and a sudden gust of wind buffeted the vehicle. Knife Man scowled and pulled out a pistol, pointing it at her. She struggled to keep her composure and her balance as pressure built behind her eyes. She couldn't just do nothing, but breaking down would not improve her situation, and she blinked to keep her eyes clear.

"Don't do anythin' rash, dearie," Knife Man sneered.

The other man put his head out the window and called up to the driver. When he came back in, he shook his head at Knife Man. Maria watched, dumbfounded, as the second man then, of all things, climbed out of the coach. Through the window! While it was moving! She had never heard of such a thing, and the scandalized face of Doña Olivia flashed through her mind. Maria almost smiled, afraid that if she did, she would start laughing hysterically.

The coach jerked sideways again and bounced crazily over the road as the horses were whipped to a greater speed. Maria braced herself, focused on keeping her seat. She clung to whatever she could for stability. Then she heard something that froze her blood.

The crack of a gunshot.

The sound echoed across the valley, and Maria huddled into the corner, trying to make herself too small to attract further danger. Cursing came from above, and another gunshot. Both shots had come from behind the coach. Had someone come after her? She tried to cower down further, but the bouncing and jolting kept her from doing more than tightening her grip. Knife Man never took his gaze, or the aim of his gun, off her.

A deafening crack of gunfire from the coach startled Maria, followed by a third shot from behind.

174

Her heart raced as she listened, trying to piece together what was happening outside the covered windows. For several heartbeats she heard nothing but the pounding of hooves and creak of the wood. Suddenly, the heavy breathing of a galloping horse sounded beside the coach. The clang of swords just beyond the door made her breath catch in her throat.

Knife Man turned from her to look at the door, the pistol's aim dropping. Not thinking, Maria lunged at him. He saw her coming, and her head exploded with the impact of the pistol-holding fist. Her head hit the back of the coach with a crack, and she flopped to the rocking floor. The world spun as darkness closed over her mind.

***

Miguel pulled on the reins, slowing the team to a smooth trot, certain they were out of pistol range of the men he'd dumped overboard. He should stop the coach and check on Maria. But what if one of the men found Miguel's discarded mount and came after them? He couldn't risk it. But what if she was hurt? He gritted his teeth and flicked the reins, refusing to allow the next logical question. If she was hurt, the best thing would be to get her home as quickly as possible.

The coach rocked abruptly, and Miguel spun, his pistol out, expecting to see someone climbing onto the coach as he'd done. A woman's muffled cry came from inside, followed by a thud that rocked the vehicle and made Miguel's heart leap into his throat. He violently pulled the horses to a stop and jumped down before the team had stopped entirely. His blood ran cold at the muffled sound of a pistol shot. The world around him seemed to slow as his feet hit the ground and he pulled his cutlass from its sheath. He knew full well the sword would be no use against a pistol, but his own pistols had been spent. He had to get to Maria.

He raised his sword and threw open the door, jumping back, ready to swing at whatever came through the door. The rest of the world fell away as he waited one heartbeat. Then another. No longer willing to wait for fate, he rushed forward. And froze as time and the world stilled around him.

A large man slumped against Maria. Viciously, Miguel grabbed him with his free hand and yanked him away from her, throwing him onto the dirt beneath the coach. He landed with a dull thud, but didn't move.

Miguel turned back to Maria, and his heart stilled. She was covered in blood, staring lifelessly into space. He reached for her and her head jerked up, wild-eyed. Her shaking hands, holding a pistol, lurched upward, aiming the weapon at him. She pulled the trigger, and the empty flintlock clicked.

He stared at her as she trembled, her face wet with tears, and his mind caught up with the fact that he had not been shot. Slowly, he pulled himself into the coach.

"Shhhh, Maria, it's me. It's Miguel," he crooned, reaching toward her. "It's all right. I'm here now; everything's going to be fine. Can you give me the pistol?" He gently touched her hand, and she dropped

176

the gun as though it had burned her. Without letting go
of her hand or breaking eye contact, he reached down
and picked up the pistol, tucking it into his coat. "Are
you hurt?"

Maria shook her head abruptly, and Miguel took a
seat beside her on the floorboards. Gently, he pulled her
hands toward her lap and wrapped his other arm around
her shoulders. She rocked stiffly back and forth, and he
pulled her head down onto his shoulder. She melted
into him and sobbed.

"Shhhh, it's all right, *mi querida*, you're safe now,
I'm here." He pulled her onto his lap, rocking her as she
whimpered in his arms. The weight of her warm body
anchored him, and for a moment, nothing existed
beyond the walls of the coach. Gently, he wiped away
the worst of the blood.

The sound of approaching horses brought Miguel
back to himself. He reached for his cutlass, lying on the
seat beside him. Pulling Maria more firmly to him with
one arm, he raised the weapon to strike as the door
burst open. A familiar figure abruptly stopped in the
doorway, and Miguel paused.

Don Ciro stood still, torn between reaching for his
blood-covered daughter, and the threat of the man who
held her. Slowly, Ciro lowered the pistol he'd brought,
and Miguel lowered the cutlass, wrapping his sword
arm protectively over Maria.

"Is she hurt?" Don Ciro asked in a low voice.

Miguel shook his head and Ciro backed out.

Someone climbed into the driver's seat, and the carriage started to move. As he rested his head on Maria's hair, Miguel could hear the horses surrounding them. Maria continued to cling to him, and eventually, her sobs stilled. She pulled away a little and looked up at him.

"Miguel?" she whispered.

"I'm here, Maria," he said.

"Don't ever leave me again," she pleaded, returning her face to his shirt, clinging to his coat.

"I won't, *mi morena*, I'll always be right here for you." He held her tighter until they pulled up to the Álvarez home.

Ciro opened the door, the torchlight of the *hacienda* lighting the drive. He reached for Maria, who had fallen asleep. Ignoring him, Miguel shifted one hand beneath her knees and stood, unwilling to give her up, even to her father. She stirred as Ciro helped Miguel down from the coach with his bundle but didn't wake, only clinging tighter to Miguel's coat. Before Ciro could say anything, Miguel strode toward the house. He would see her safe. Ciro took a step to follow but hesitated, then turned back to his men, giving orders for securing the *hacienda* for the evening.

***

Nana opened the door to Maria's room as Miguel brought her up. "I'll take her," the old woman said firmly, but Miguel brushed past her without breaking his stride.

Somewhat flustered, Maria's old nursemaid bolted in front of him and turned down the bed. Miguel laid her down, but as he pulled away Maria's hand shot out and grabbed his wrist.

"Don't go," she whispered, looking up at him.

"I won't," he promised.

Nana sighed and pulled over a chair for him to sit on. She grumbled about young love and hearts and promises as she fussed over Maria, wiping her hands and face clean and constantly forcing Miguel to move his chair further away.

The blatant domesticity of the situation relaxed Miguel, allowing the full weight of what had happened to settle over him. She had been taken. Because of him. When Nana had finally done all she could to get Maria dressed down with Miguel there, she turned on him with her hands on her hips.

"If you're not going to leave, you're to face out the window," Nana said, pointing.

Miguel leaned over Maria and whispered in her ear, "I'm not leaving, but I am going to go sit over there. I promise I won't leave."

"I'm not an idiot, you know. I heard her," Maria tried to joke, but it came out in a shaky mumble.

Miguel almost smiled. He turned his chair to the window, leaning out over the sill to cut off his peripheral vision. He could still hear, though, as Nana stood Maria up and helped her remove her dress and corset. What might have happened if he hadn't found her? The thought oppressed him, pushing his heart through the floor.

The rustle of the Maria's nightdress dropping over her and the creak of her bed as she returned to it seemed to accuse him. Had he picked the wrong route she would not be here to make those noises. Nana pulled the covers up the bed again, tucking them around Maria. Miguel hadn't even been able to protect her; she'd had to shoot her captor herself.

The moment Nana stepped away, Miguel was back beside the bed, holding Maria's hand and moving a curl of hair from her face. She smiled up at him.

"Go to sleep. I'll be here," he whispered.

She closed her eyes and her breathing slowed.

Footsteps at the door pulled Miguel's attention. Ciro stood there watching them, a pain in his eyes.

Nana let out an unabashed sigh of exasperation. "She needs to rest," Nana insisted as Ciro entered the room, taking a place beside Miguel. "No need to listen to me," she muttered as she set about putting away Maria's things and picking up the discarded red dress.

As Maria's breath settled into the deep rhythm of sleep, Ciro motioned for Miguel to follow him. Inevitability hung over him like death's scythe. Miguel looked at Maria, hesitant, his hand entwined with hers.

"I'll be right outside the door, *mi morena*. I'll be here," he whispered into her ear and let go of her hand. She stirred a little, but when he was sure she would not wake, he walked out into the hall with Ciro, who gently closed the door behind them.

"What happened?" he demanded, not quite able to hide his anger.

"I, we … had a fight. She'd noticed that I'm always following her and demanded that I leave her alone. I thought it best to give her some space," he said, too ashamed of his stupidity to meet Ciro's eyes. "I should never have left her, never have let her out of my sight."

"She should have been safe there," Ciro growled. "Olivia's men should have been watching her. *My* men were supposed to be watching her."

"One of your men in Doña Olivia's employ came to warn me. Someone had ordered that all eyes be removed from your daughter. I shouldn't have let her out of my sight." Miguel slumped again, sitting heavily on a chair that he was certain had not been there before. This was it then, the moment he had sworn he would never allow again. But this time, the exile would be his own fault. This time, it would be deserved.

"This is intolerable." Ciro growled to himself, pacing. "Unforgivable."

Intolerable. Miguel nodded. Unforgivable. There were not more appropriate words. Miguel stood and started down the hall. It was late, but he would certainly be able to find a ship to take him before the tide turned.

Ciro put his hand on Miguel's chest, halting him. "Where do you think you're going?" Ciro asked, not unkindly.

"Away from here. She's right. All I do is bring her trouble. You're right, it was unforgivable. She'll never forgive me …." Miguel didn't have the heart to continue or to fight Ciro as he pushed him back into the chair.

"Miguel, you are staying right here, where you promised you would be. People make mistakes; it is not you with whom I am angry. And neither is she. I will need you here with me, with her, now more than ever. I can't believe Gonza would go this far. Things are going to get ugly soon, and she will need you while I am gone."

***

Ciro knew that Miguel did not hear him, but he was convinced now that Miguel wouldn't leave. He strode down the hall, pulling at his cravat. Events would move faster now, he was sure of it. He would need to prepare. Eventually, he would need to leave, and if he was lucky, things would not come to a head before he could see his daughter securely provided for.

Chapter 14

MARIA STOOD in a field some distance from Maracaibo, the nearby jungle dark and swaying in the stormy breeze. The sky overhead was a deep indigo and drenched with stars, and she could smell the impending rain. But then, it always rained here.

She wrapped her arms about herself and shivered. *It's just the cold,* she tried to tell herself. *Not nerves, just cold.*

The shadowed jungle whispered to her, unheard voices urging her toward it. In the distance she could hear hoofbeats, shouting, and the crack of a gunshot. Maria's heart raced as she spun, trying to locate the sound as it bore down upon her, surrounding her.

Suddenly, there he was.

Alistair! Maria fell on his neck, hugging him to her. He nuzzled her for a moment before nudging her up. As she stood, the sound faded, both the hoofbeats and the jungle's whispers. A fresh breeze, thick with the storm's scent, pushed Maria's hair back from her face as Alistair urged her away from the jungle.

As she clung to his collar, he pulled her forward through the wind, and she fell forward into less chaotic dreams.

***

Maria woke from a restless sleep with the lingering memory of dark dreams. Her head pounded, and she groaned at the multitude of aches that flared to life as she rolled onto her back. The morning sunlight slanted into her room through the open windows, carrying birdsong on its back. She closed her eyes again, but darkness and a flash of light played against her eyelids, and suddenly the weight of her quilt was suffocating. With a shudder, she opened her eyes. She needed to get up, anyhow.

Maria sat up, pushing back the offending blankets despite protesting muscles. Stretching her back, she rubbed her hands over her face with a yawn but froze at the sight of something that should most definitely not have been in her room, let alone while she'd been sleeping. Miguel was asleep in a chair beside her bed.

Maria hesitated, her hand hovering over her quilt as she weighed her options. He looked so peaceful, so beautiful asleep, with the sunlight lying across his still form. But she had an increasingly urgent need to get up. She glanced around the room for her robe. It sat several feet away, draped over her dressing table chair. Maria gave it a rueful look. There was no hope for it. The only way to get the robe would be to chance his waking as she snuck over to it. Maria bit her lip. She had no idea what kind of a sleeper he was. The choice lay before her—bodily necessity or decency? With a sigh, she flopped back down onto her pillows, pulled the blankets back over herself, and turned toward him again.

Miguel's head rested against the wall with his face turned toward her, relaxed and peaceful. A bit of his messy, dark hair fell into his face. He'd removed his coat and bunched it behind his head as a makeshift pillow. Maria's eyes travelled down to his chest, which rose and fell with his deep, even breaths. He still wore the fancy shirt from the night before, and his hands rested oddly at his waist. It made her smile to note that one hand covered the butt of a pistol lying on his lap, and the other was on his cutlass.

She had always seen the cutlass—he was never without it—but she'd only occasionally seen him carry a pistol. The sound of a gunshot from behind echoed in her memory and set her heart beating faster. The urge to turn away and hide beneath her covers pulled at her, but at the same time, the idea of the weighty quilt draped over her repelled her. *I'm home. I'm safe here.* Maria gritted her teeth and forced herself to breathe slowly. She had not imagined then that it was Miguel who had come after her. But the pistol on his lap was disturbingly familiar, and somehow, she knew it wasn't his.

She shook her head to dispel the creeping foreboding and lay back on the pillows, trying to think of something else. Her body assisted in the effort, demanding to be relieved. She stared at the ceiling for a few minutes more, hoping for a solution. Maybe Nana would come in and solve her problem for her. With a sigh of resignation, Maria accepted that the decision was hers. She'd either have to wake Miguel or walk across the room in front of him in her nightdress to get the robe herself. As appreciative of him as she was, that was just too much.

"Miguel," she whispered sotto voce.

He shifted in his chair but didn't wake.

"Migueeeeel," she said again, this time a little louder. When he still didn't wake she grinned.

Maria reached behind her and grabbed one of her pillows by the corner. "Migueeeelll, you really ought to wake up now." She swung the pillow around and let it fly at Miguel's head.

Miguel's eyes flew open just as the pillow hit him square in the face. He leapt to his feet, knocking the pillow away with the pistol and drawing his cutlass all in the same graceful movement. Before the pillow hit the floor, Miguel was poised, ready for combat. Maria's breath caught for a moment at the beauty of it—she'd never seen him move like that, stand like that. For the first time, she truly saw in him the powerful and dangerous man that he was, and a deep feeling she couldn't define filled her. Then she started to giggle.

He looked over at her, puzzled, then down at the pillow. He sheathed his sword with a sheepish grin and tucked the pistol into his belt. Maria tried to come up with an appropriate quip, but before she could, the door of her room opened. Nana bustled into the room with a tray of food, followed by a short trail of servants with buckets of steaming bath water.

"Ah, you're awake," she chirped, nodding to the others to fill the short tub in the adjoining room. "Feeling well, too, by the looks of things." She gave Miguel an appraising look; a defensive aura still radiated from him. Nana raised an eyebrow at the pillow on the floor.

"It would appear that Maria's room has become infested with flying pillows," he said gravely to her, and Maria covered her mouth to hide her mirth. "This one attacked me while I slept, but I taught it to mind its manners." He picked it up and handed it to Maria, who gave an abashed smile under Nana's reproving look.

"There is breakfast for you in the kitchen, Miguel," Nana said kindly. When he hesitated she added, "Maria can't get washed and dressed while you're here. I'll ensure her safety from vagrant pillows while you are gone."

Maria blushed at her nursemaid's candidness and Miguel hastened out, embarrassed.

Maria watched his back until the door was shut, then turned to Nana. "Thank goodness you came when you did. I need to relieve myself, but my dress robe was on the other side of the room, and I couldn't get Miguel to wake up so that I could get it!" She tried to hop out of bed, but her sore muscles protested anything related to quick movements. She hobbled across the room to her privy.

Once relieved, Maria eased herself into a warm bath, grateful for the heat against her sore muscles.

"That was no way to treat him, Maria," Nana scolded her as she scrubbed and untangled Maria's hair.

"There was no harm done, and we both had a good laugh," Maria said with a shrug, her mind reviewing the way he had looked, jumping to her defense, his eyes dark and the line of his back and shoulders beneath his shirt …. She blushed, forcing her mind elsewhere.

"It was unkind. That man saved your life last night and has refused to leave your side since. He deserves your respect, if nothing else," Nana chided.

Maria stared at the water in silence. Once again, she had chosen wrong and hurt someone she cared for in the process. She ought to have just waited for Nana.

After a few minutes, Nana urged her to finish bathing quickly, as Miguel would certainly be returning. Encouraged by the thought, Maria moved as fast as her sore muscles would allow, surprised at how much better they felt after soaking in the warm water.

Once she was dressed and her hair in order, Maria sat down to the breakfast Nana had brought. Maria set her mother's necklace on the table beside her and inspected the red stone as she pushed the food around on her plate, uninterested in eating.

"What is this?" Maria asked Nana.

"Your mother's necklace. Goodness, child, I knew you bumped your head but I didn't think you'd lost your memory as well."

Maria laughed. "I know it's my mother's necklace. I meant, what is this stone? Why did my mother always wear it?"

"Ah. These old ears don't hear as well as they used to. I can't do the things I used to, my poor old body creaks with every movement. Why, when I was young—"

"Nana! The stone?" Maria feigned exasperation.

"Ah, yes. It's red jasper, *chica*. It is called *tu'uma* by the Wayuu, the natives to the north, and considered by them to be extremely precious. Your mother always wore it because it was her mother's, and her mother's before that. It is generations old, older than even I am, and that's saying something." Nana's eyes twinkled.

Maria spun the stone in its setting as she ate, watching the way it reflected the light. She looked up at a knock on the door, and found Miguel. He'd changed into clean clothes and his well-worn coat. He still wore his cutlass, but the pistols were either gone or hidden. A moment of disappointment hit Maria at the sight of his tidied hair; she preferred the lock of hair in his face. She held up the necklace, and he smiled, coming into the room. As he took it from her hands, their fingertips brushed, and she looked away, lifting her hair from her neck. He draped the necklace over her throat, and the feel of his gentle fingers on her skin sent a thrill down her spine.

"*Muchas gracias*, Miguel." Maria looked over her shoulder to him when he dropped his hands.

"It was my pleasure," Miguel responded in English.

Maria looked at him quizzically, not sure that she'd correctly understood. Uncomfortable with the way he stood above her, she stood with as much grace as she could muster, only to come to an abrupt halt when that put her face to face with him. Her mind went blank as she looked into his green eyes, the space between their bodies tangible. Had she ever stood so close to him? She forgot how to breathe, and her mouth went dry. She licked her lips, and her eyes travelled down his face, along his clean-shaven jaw to his mouth. She could practically feel the short space between them, and her hands ached to close the distance. But did she dare? She glanced back up at his eyes, but the intensity of his gaze made her look down, tracing the line of his shoulder and down his arm. As she reached for him, he leaned closer to her, and she closed her eyes, drawing in a breath.

Nana cleared her throat, and the world slammed back into Maria's senses.

They jerked apart and promptly found objects of interest in very separate parts of the room, stuttering their apologies. Miguel fidgeted with the coat he'd left on a chair as Maria went to her mirror and played with some trinkets, her face on fire and her body tingling.

Miguel regained his composure before she did and turned to her, his words tumbling over themselves. "Well, you had an exciting evening. I'll let you get back to your rest."

"I'm plenty rested, thank you." Maria attempted to force herself to be calm. Despite her embarrassment, she was not yet ready for him to leave. "I want to walk in the gardens, if you'll accompany me." She held out her elbow.

Miguel turned to Nana. She merely gave them an amused smile.

"Are you sure? You look so tired still ...." Miguel hesitated.

"I assure you, I am fine." Maria held her up head and started toward the door, ignoring her protesting muscles. "If you won't come with me, I'll go on my own." She stopped in the doorway and gave a mischievous smile over her shoulder. "But, if you don't come with me, I don't know that I shall ever be able to take you at your word again."

"I don't think I could live with that ...." Miguel murmured and followed Maria, putting his arm around her waist with the pretense of assisting her down the hall.

Nana watched them go from the doorway as Ciro came down the hall.

"They'll be good together, I think," Nana said to him.

Ciro nodded absently and looked at the old woman. "Why do you stay with us?" he asked. "Maria's too old to still need a nursemaid."

"I stay because she asked me to stay, among other reasons." Nana gave an enigmatic smile.

"That's no answer, Nana. Surely you have a family of your own. What is your real name, anyhow?"

"This has ever been my family, and Nana is the only name I want." She turned back into the young woman's room to straighten it up.

Ciro looked on, pondering on all the strange things that made up his life.

***

Maria tried not to flinch as she walked, but Miguel could tell she hurt. That she was more tired than she let on was apparent when she slowed near a bench in a more secluded part of the garden.

"Shall we sit?" He gestured to the stone bench.

She smiled up at him and sat, sagging slightly as she arranged her skirts. "It's odd," she said as he sat, careful to place a proper distance between them. Maria held her hands in her lap, and he was acutely aware of how easy it would be to take her hand if she let it fall to the side.

"What is?" he asked.

"I ache all over, all across my back and shoulders, and my head too, of course." Maria smoothed out her skirt. "It's certainly not the first time I've been in a fast-moving coach, and probably not the bumpiest ride I've been on, but this is so much worse, and I can't fathom why."

"Are you sure you're ready to talk about last night?" Miguel asked, his voice soft. He wished he could put his arm around her without upsetting her.

"What do you mean?" She didn't look up at him.

Miguel hesitated. He shouldn't push her; but he had to know what she thought about him. "What do you remember about last night?"

He regretted his words as soon as they were out of his mouth. What if she remembered what had happened on the balcony? What if she hated him for it? What if she, rightfully, blamed him for what had happened?

"I remember those villains forcing me into a coach, a lot of bouncing around, hearing some gunshots, and then ..." She hesitated and blushed. "... being in your arms and just ... feeling safe."

An insufferable joy that she felt safe with him warred with trepidation as he forced himself to ask, "What do you remember of the ball?"

"I had a fairly good time. I remember lots of lights, lovely gowns, and then walking outside. The whole evening is pretty fuzzy, but I imagine it was an effect of all the excitement." She smiled warmly at him.

Loathing himself for his cowardice, he didn't press her any further. Instead, he reached over and took her hand. It was warm and soft and fit perfectly in his. She smiled at him, giving him the courage to wrap his other arm around her. She leaned into him, resting her head on his shoulder. Feelings of warmth and peace rose into his chest, held there by the calming weight of her head. Her soft, glossy black hair pressed against his neck and chin, and he ached to stroke it. Mostly, he wanted to pull her into his arms as he had the night before and hold her tight, but the spell that had fallen over them seemed too fragile for movement.

So they stayed as they were and said nothing more, afraid that once the moment had passed it might never come again.

Chapter 15

T HE CHIMING FROM the grandfather clock down the hall sounded the lateness of the hour, muffled and quiet despite the silence of the sleeping household. Miguel shifted his weight and did a mental check of his weapons, running through various techniques of attack, both proper and unsavory. Growing up around the hard crewmen of his father's merchant ship had given him a well-rounded education when it came to fighting.

Footsteps down the hall reached Miguel's ears. Even, heavy, and nearly silent. Don Ciro, then, come to relieve him of his vigil at Maria's door. Miguel rolled his shoulders, working the tension from them and his back. The old man needed his rest; there was no reason Miguel couldn't stay all night.

The old crone, Nana, hadn't allowed him back into Maria's room after the first night, and as much as he hated to admit it, she was right. It had been entirely improper, but there was nothing improper about him guarding her outside her door. More importantly, he knew she felt more secure with him there.

"*Buenas noches*, Miguel," Ciro said softly as he approached.

"Evening, Don Ciro." Miguel nodded to the other man.

"Another long night standing guard?" Ciro came to a stop across the hall from Miguel and leaned against the wall. "When do you sleep?"

"I could ask the same of you, sir. You've come to take my place, and it is not even midnight. Don't think I haven't noticed you come a few minutes earlier each evening."

Don Ciro nodded, dropping his hands casually into the pockets of his robe. "How is she?"

"She doesn't sleep well if I'm not here and won't leave the *hacienda* without me nearby."

"But at least she's going out again. I should think you wouldn't need to guard her door every night any more. It has been nearly two weeks, and nothing has happened. I have people in place here to ensure her safety."

"Like you did at Casa de la Cuesta?" Miguel realized his impertinence as soon as the words were out of his mouth, but he refused to take them back, standing up straighter.

"No, not like Casa de la Cuesta. Sergio is … an easy man sometimes. He does not keep as tight a rein on his business as he probably should. But every man here, and woman, too, is loyal to the Álvarez family. Especially where Gonza is concerned."

"You're still convinced it's him, then?" Miguel shifted his weight again and mimicked his employer's posture, draping his hand over the pommel of his cutlass.

"He's as much as admitted it." Ciro looked down the hall and sighed. "Miguel, he wants something from me. I'd do anything to protect my daughter, but this is a thing I simply cannot give."

"So the goal was to take her and force you to do … what?"

Ciro brought his eyes to Miguel's as a fierceness settled over his features. "What do you know of the history of the natives to the north? The Wayuu?"

The Wayuu? What did they have to do with any of this? "Maria mentioned them to me once, said there had been a few rebellions in the past. She didn't figure there would be more trouble with them. Why?"

"I am a man of peace, and a man of business. But I have in the past, been a man of war. Gonza would have me be so again." Ciro shook his head. "But not as an honest soldier, no. He cares nothing for the cause, or the lives, or the cost of human souls. All he sees is that there is money to be made, and he wants me to support him in this.

"There are rumors of discontent in both the city and the villages. Tensions between the Spanish and the natives are growing. Rather than try to find peace, people like Gonza fan those sparks, pushing them into flames just to see the world burn so they may forge their fortunes in the furnace of destruction."

Miguel nodded as the pieces fell into place. "And if you publicly supported it, another war would come that much faster."

Ciro stood up straight from the wall and crossed to Miguel. "But more than that, I would be selling out my soul and everything that I've ever held of value."

"Does Gonza by himself really have enough influence to push things that far?"

"I'm certain that he doesn't. He's conniving, but this maneuvering … it just doesn't quite feel right. There has to be someone else guiding his steps …." Ciro shook his head. "I'm sure it's nothing."

Miguel raised his eyebrow at him, skeptical. "Is this supposed to reassure me?"

Ciro put his hand on Miguel's shoulder. Miguel held back his immediate impulse to shake it off. He still wished he'd broken the arm of the last man to do so, but Don Ciro was different. Miguel waited.

"Here's the thing, Miguel. I'm getting the impression you've about made up your mind to stay here permanently." Ciro paused, watching Miguel.

Miguel stood straighter, glancing at Maria's door, then back to Ciro.

"If that's the case, then I have plans that need to be put into motion. My first concern is, as always, Maria's safety and future. To that end, I believe it is time you start taking a greater part in the running of this business. For that, you will need to sleep."

Uncertainty filled Miguel. Once before he had been robbed of everything he'd held dear by a man he'd always believed he could trust. Now, before him stood another man who had been a complete stranger not so long ago, offering to bring him in, asking for his trust. Or was Ciro using him, too? Was it worth the risk?

The warm wood of Maria's door frame pressed into Miguel's back. For her, though, he would risk anything.

"She doesn't sleep well if I don't stay," Miguel repeated.

"You can stay until she is asleep." Ciro pulled Miguel away from the door. "Go to your room and sleep. She will be fine, and you will be more use to her rested."

Reluctantly, Miguel walked away.

***

Maria stood just outside the door to the main house of the *hacienda*, watching the coach roll up, a sick feeling she couldn't define settling in her stomach. The footman opened the door of the coach and a thin, dark man stepped out. Well-dressed, he walked with an arrogant stride that struck Maria as distasteful. She shrank back, hiding behind the nearest arching pillar of the arcade as the man swept up the steps.

"Senior Gonza," the doorman said, holding his hand out for the man's hat and leading him in. "If you will wait here, I will inform Don Álvarez of your presence."

Gonza. She had overheard her father speak of this man more than once, and often with contempt. She watched him from the doorway, and when he looked up and met her eye, it made her skin crawl. She stood straighter, holding up her chin. Even if nothing else seemed certain in her life right now, she could still hold herself with pride.

"Maria," Miguel called from the courtyard. Gonza gave her a cruel smile as she met his gaze. "Maria, I've got the horses—" Miguel cut off as he neared and saw Gonza in the foyer

Gonza's smile turned absolutely feral and Maria narrowed her eyes at him. Miguel put his hand on her elbow, his grip gentle but tense. Maria turned her back on the intruder, sweeping out into the sunlight and the saddled horses that awaited them. The knots in her stomach loosened with each step.

Despite Miguel's steadying hand on her back, Maria trembled as she reached her horse. For the first time in weeks, she found herself relieved to leave the *hacienda*. "I don't know what it is about that man, but I don't like him in my home."

Miguel put his hands on her waist and helped her into her saddle. "Neither do I, and I do know what it is I don't like about him. He's an absolute scoundrel. If I'd known he was coming, we'd have left sooner."

Maria gathered her reins and watched Miguel swing himself awkwardly up into his saddle. She smiled. He tried so hard, but it was clear he was not meant to be a horseman.

"Are you sure you're ready for this?" he asked as they walked their horses through the gates.

200

Maria's stomach twisted at the thought. "My father likes to say that it is better to get a painful thing over with quickly. When he was teaching me to ride when I was small, I once fell off my horse. I was terrified to get back on, but he told me the longer I waited, the worse it would be. And even worse, the horse knows when you're afraid and will act out. He always made me get back on the horse as soon as possible. So whether I'm ready or not, it's time to get back on this horse."

"Is there any life problem your father's wisdom can't fix?" Miguel asked with a laugh as the *hacienda*'s gates passed out of sight.

"Pain," Maria said quickly. "He says that pain has to be passed through."

"Unless you pass out." Miguel's eyes twinkled.

Maria laughed. She loved the way he always made her laugh, even when she was upset. Especially when she was upset. Her world had been shaken to its core. She'd always known there were evil people out there, but it had always seemed like such an academic thing. Something to read about in books. But to have it reach out and snatch her from her life, from a place she'd always considered a home ... Maria shuddered despite the morning heat.

"Are you sure you're all right with this?" Miguel leaned over and squeezed her hand, bumping his knee against her horse as he did so. "I can take you home and send your excuses to the Señoritas de la Cuesta."

"It will be fine." She squeezed his hand in return, then let it go. "It's time I went back there. Besides, that awful man might still be meeting with my father, and I don't have any interest in being within a mile of him, if possible. Besides, it is nice to spend some time alone with you. I feel you're so busy now, we hardly ever have time to talk."

Miguel gave her a rueful smile. "Your father's decided he wants to bring me on more fully in the business. I almost think he had hopes to do so from the beginning. I was raised on a merchant ship, the son of a merchant captain after all."

Maria gave him a playful shove. "You never told me that! What were you doing as a simple deckhand in *La Solidad*?"

"That's a story for another day. The point is, though, I'm sorry I haven't been around for you as much as I'd have liked."

The knowledge that he liked being around her warmed her, and she used it to combat the chill of anxiety that crept up her spine as they neared the plantation. When they arrived, Miguel walked into the house with her instead of making his excuses and leaving.

Doña Olivia greeted them warmly, as though nothing untoward had ever happened. She then insisted that Maria and Miguel stay to dine that morning, though she herself had other business to attend. Doña Olivia directed them to one of the balconies where her daughters and niece were enjoying the nice weather as they ate. Walking through the familiar halls felt strange to Maria, as though something as normal as this was

202

from a distant past, almost another lifetime. The girls greeted her, all aflutter as Maria came to the table. Betania was her usual warm self, and Selena as well. Elisa, however, went straight for Miguel.

Maria felt her smile turn forced as Elisa fawned over Miguel.

"How have you been? You're looking so well. How fine that coat looks on you."

Why not just throw yourself in his arms and pet his face? Maria maneuvered herself to stand between them, gratified at the way Miguel pointedly ignored Elisa.

"Have a seat won't you, Elisa?" Maria gestured to the table where Selena and Betania had already taken their seats.

"Oh, of course. I was just so excited to have you here again. It has simply been *ages,* and there is just so much to say." Elisa set herself down as daintily as a blossom on water, conveniently beside the open seat Miguel had moved toward. Miguel changed directions, and, after helping Maria with her chair, sat as far from Elisa as the small table would allow.

They chatted for a few minutes of menial things, but Maria felt out of place, as though watching the whole thing from a distance. Miguel's presence beside her, however, lent her reassurance.

"What do you suppose Selena is so antsy about?" Miguel whispered, nodding toward the anxiously bouncing girl.

"Probably has ants biting her ankles," Maria whispered back, hiding a smile in her teacup.

203

"You should put her out of her misery and ask her what is on her mind."

"Selena—" Maria started as soon as the conversation lulled.

"Maria! You'll never guess what has happened with Betania!" she exclaimed.

"Selena!" Betania blushed, but obviously wanting her to continue.

"What? What's going on?" Maria looked between the two of them.

"Well, remember that boy, Benito Garcia—" Elisa started before Selena could say anything.

"He's not a boy," Betania objected.

"—the one we were debating whether to invite or not?" Elisa continued without missing a beat.

Maria nodded. "Yes, he danced with Betania almost the whole night."

"Well, it turns out they've been courting behind our backs!" Selena said.

Maria wasn't surprised but wondered where Betania found the time; it seemed she was almost always with her sister and cousin. But then again, Maria hadn't been around as much recently.

"We've become engaged," Betania murmured, giving Maria a knowing smile.

"Congratulations!" Miguel raised his cup to her.

"Yes, that's wonderful, Betania!" Maria returned the smile, though she could tell Betania was uncomfortable with the attention.

"Tell us, Maria, what happened to you that night?" Betania asked, clearly desperate to change the subject. "You just disappeared, and no one seemed to know where you were."

Maria shrank back from the question, her mind blank as she felt four sets of eyes on her. Miguel rested his hand on her arm, calming her and she looked up at him.

"We're rather curious to hear what you've heard." He turned the question back to them without looking toward Maria. Maria remained tense as they started talking.

"Well, oddly, none of the servants know anything about it," Betania said.

"Only you would care for servant's gossip." Elisa snorted.

"I saw you leave. It looked like you two were having a fight," Selena offered quietly, looking toward them for some sign of affirmation. At Miguel's nod she smiled and continued. "Doña Olivia told us that you left in your carriage, but that your coachman had indulged in too much drink—"

"Shameful, but what else could you expect from a *mestizo* servant?" Elisa cut in, and Miguel shot her an angry look.

"Worried, your faithful sea dog followed you on horseback and rescued you from the runaway carriage," Selena finished, with Miguel bristling at the reference to himself that he had come to despise.

"So romantic." Betania sighed.

Maria was unsure if Betania was referring to the tale or her new fiancé. When Maria realized that none of them knew what had happened, she relaxed a little, but something about the way Elisa was looking at Miguel made her wary. There was a maliciousness hiding in the set of her lips and a sparkle of jealousy in her hazel eyes.

"Did you know why she and her pup were fighting?" Elisa asked in a low voice, leaning toward Selena.

"No, do tell!" Selena demanded, excited for more gossip.

Dread settled over Maria. She only vaguely remembered that they had fought, but she couldn't quite recall what it had been about.

"Really, it's not something to be discussed," Miguel cut in, sensing Maria's growing agitation.

Elisa's eyes darted from Maria to Miguel at the questioning look that passed between them and continued with venom lacing her words.

"It would seem that puppy Miguel had finally come to his senses and tried to remove himself from Maria's leash. He wanted to be alone with me, you see. So, he took me out to the balcony, that one over there." She pointed.

"Elisa, perhaps you'd better not," Betania stated as Miguel glowered at her sister.

Maria shook her head, confused. There had been something about the balcony. What was it?

"Why ever not, dear sister? There's no harm in the truth," Elisa said with a dainty shrug.

"I think we should leave." Miguel stood and gently took Maria's arm to help her up.

Maria stood slowly and looked at Elisa, searching her memory for the truth. Elisa had never been one to be trusted with the truth.

Elisa looked back into Maria's eyes and continued, pouting. "He took me to the balcony, where it was dark and he thought we were alone. He told me that he loved me, that he wanted to always be with me."

"That's a lie," Miguel hissed, and took a menacing step toward Elisa, his hand going to his sword hilt.

She sat calmly and lifted a cup of tea to her lips, glaring into his eyes. She sipped her tea without breaking eye contact and then continued.

"Then, he pushed me up against the wall, whispering into my ear, and kissed my neck, right here." She pointed to her jaw and Selena gasped, scandalized. Then Elisa turned her eyes to Maria, her voice as sweet as honey. "But then Maria came and beckoned him away, and, like a good little dog he followed, ready for his beating."

In a flash, Maria remembered. She remembered seeing them together, seeing him leaning over Elisa, leaning down to her. Maria felt heat rise in her chest, but she didn't have the strength to push it away so she turned and fled.

Miguel gave one last glare at Elisa, finally cowing her, and stalked out after Maria.

"That was cruel, Elisa. Look at what you have done," he heard Betania chide.

"That was the idea," Elisa said coldly, and Miguel quickened his pace.

***

Maria waited for him at the front of the house, watching for their horses to be brought around. Her emotions swirled around her. Elisa had meant to make her upset. Elisa twisted things to get what she wanted. She wanted Maria upset. This was nothing new, but Elisa had never been so vicious about it. Nor so successful.

Miguel walked up behind her and touched her arm. "Maria ...." he said, a note of pleading in his voice

"Not now, not here, please." She pulled away. She needed to figure this out. For the moment, though, what she knew without a doubt was that she wouldn't give Elisa the satisfaction of dealing with it here. She would not be Elisa's entertainment.

Miguel backed away a little, certain she could still feel him there, behind her. When the groom brought their horses, she mounted and started off at a trot, not waiting for Miguel. He quickly caught up to her, but she didn't speak.

The silence grew between them as Miguel fought down his anger at Elisa's cruelty. And what if Maria was unforgiving? No matter what it took, he would make sure she heard his side, but what then? What if she wanted nothing more to do with him? He tightened his grip on the reins and his gelding tossed his head. His fear circled around again to anger, each emotion vying for control. He struggled to balance them, knowing that if either won they would remove reason from his grasp.

Maria was caught in a whirlwind of conflicting emotions of her own. Elisa was a liar. But Maria remembered it. The balcony, the music, the faded evening light. The sense of betrayal. But Miguel *cared* for her, didn't he? Why would Elisa lie? Maria had grown up with the girl, they were practically sisters. Why would Elisa be so hateful?

They slowed their horses to a walk as the plantation disappeared behind them, more of that night coming back in bits and flashes. She and Miguel had argued, and she wasn't even sure why. Despair washed over her as she remembered his anger. It probably was only loyalty to her father that kept him around.

Miguel brought his horse abreast of Maria's, and she tried vainly to wipe away the tears on her face.

"I'm not ready to go home yet," she said, her voice thick with emotion.

"I understand," he said gently. "We need to talk, and I know a place where we should be alone." He turned down a road that led away from the town.

She nodded and followed in silence, riding between various plantations which eventually gave way to grazing pastures. Miguel led them to a glade, separate from the jungles in the distance.

As they passed into the cool shade, Maria gasped. "It's so well-manicured, almost as if one of Doña Olivia's gardens were allowed to grow at will."

Miguel nodded. "I'd never quite thought of it that way, but it does look like she came in and tried to tame the wild." They continued until they reached a little clearing with benches artfully placed in it.

"What is this place?" Maria wondered, eyeing the simply designed stone benches.

"A friend of your father grazes his sheep here, in the surrounding area. Their family has done so for three or four generations. His mother started domesticating this place when he was a child, and she was the one who brought the benches. He's kept it up since then, though it is rare anyone comes here anymore. He told me I could use it if I ever needed to 'get away' for a bit."

"It's very peaceful," Maria said, calmed by the whisper of the breeze through the trees and the cheerful chirping of birds. Something about this place made all her fears seem less potent. Miguel helped her dismount and tethered their horses to a tree. Maria moved closer to a large flowering plant with trumpet-shaped white and pale orange blossoms that she didn't recognize, as Miguel pulled a blanket from his saddlebags.

"How did you know to bring that?" she asked with a laugh as he spread it across one of the benches.

"I like to be prepared. I always bring supplies with me in case I have to spend a night somewhere."

210

"What are you talking about? You've never not come home." She gave him a sideways look, surely he was joking.

"After a life traveling the world, I like to be prepared for anything." He came to her, offering his hand, which she took. "I learned long ago that just because it hasn't happened yet doesn't mean it won't ever happen. I hate being caught unprepared." He led her to the bench and she sat. She watched him as he took a steadying breath and sat, facing her. "I wasn't prepared for you."

Maria blushed and looked away.

The silence stretched out, and Maria fidgeted with her dress, picking at imagined loose threads on the fabric.

Finally Miguel gathered his courage and gently took her hands, turning her toward him. "What Elisa said, that's not what happened."

"I wish I could believe that, Miguel, but I remember ...." She looked down at their entwined hands. It felt so right.

Miguel's heart felt weighed down with lead shot, crushing the breath from his chest. With the last bit of hope he could find he tried again. "Maria, do you trust me?"

"I don't know. I want to ...." She turned her deep brown eyes up to his. *I'm so afraid*, her eyes seemed to say.

"After we fought in the carriage, I was upset. At myself, mostly. I've been so drawn to you, Maria, since the first time I saw you." Miguel reached out and tucked a curl of hair that had fallen into her face behind her ear, and she didn't pull away. "I felt, though, that with the circumstances surrounding my employment with your father, it was inappropriate to pursue you the way I would have otherwise."

"But you followed me around anyway? How was that less inappropriate?"

A smile played on Miguel's lips. "Maria, have you ever known me to be subtle? Following you around like a lovesick puppy is not my style."

"You really hate that comparison, don't you?" She searched his face with her eyes.

Miguel leaned back, running his hand through his hair. "I ... I don't like to feel used. Or that others might think I was just using you." He turned back to Maria. "Between my close proximity to you, the nature of my responsibilities, living in your father's house, and especially his vast fortune, I knew others would believe my interest superficial. And you ... I was afraid you would never come to believe it was you I wanted and nothing else." He touched her chin, the smooth skin of her face warm in his hand, and raised her face to him.

"If it was me you wanted, why were you with Elisa?" Maria asked, her voice filled with desire to believe him.

"Maria, through those weeks when you refused to speak with me, I was drawn to you more than ever. Drawn to someone who thought of me as little more than a pet, yet just as unable to escape you. And it

212

scared me. When I saw the chance to break away from you, I took it." Maria pulled his hand away from her face and looked away, but he had to keep going. "I thought I might be able to find someone who could take my mind off you. If there was anyone in Maracaibo who could have, I knew she'd be at the ball. However, each girl I danced with couldn't compare to you. The only face I saw was yours. The only name I could remember was yours."

Maria shook her head. "That doesn't change the fact that you were there, with her on the balcony. I had been sitting in the shadows, taking a moment."

Miguel sighed. "In one last effort to get you off my mind, I sought out Elisa, but as soon as I saw her, I knew I needed to find you. I asked if she knew where you were, and she led me to the balcony. She is an unrelenting flirt and would not answer me outright."

"But I saw you. You held her against the wall and kissed ...." Maria trailed off, wanting to believe him, but unable to overcome the doubt that Elisa had planted.

"Maria, I've kissed many girls in my life. I have traveled the world and often thought myself in love, but if you believe nothing else about me, know that I have never kissed Elisa Díaz Palomo. If you can ever believe that, I have another truth to tell you."

"I want to believe it, Miguel. I want to believe that I didn't see what I thought I did. It was dark, I was tired. So much of that night is such a blur." Maria pulled her hands out of Miguel's and turned away, looking at the horses grazing serenely.

"It would appear you have two choices, then. You can believe Elisa's version of events, a girl who you know will lie to get what she wants. Or you can believe me, and I swear I didn't kiss her." Maria thought on that for a minute. Why did the confession that he had kissed other women not bother her, but the thought of Elisa even touching him made her want to slap the girl?

"What truth have you not told me?" she asked, turning back to him.

"Then you believe me?"

"For now," she said with a small smile.

"The truth then." Miguel took her hands again and leaned toward her. "The truth that I have learned since coming here and meeting you, is that I have never before known love. No one has filled my head and heart the way you have, Maria. The truth is that I love you."

Once more, time seemed to stop for Maria. *He loves me.* It was all she could think. The thought repeated itself over and over in her head as she looked into his green eyes. Then the realization struck her. *I love him.* She jerked away, standing and turning away from Miguel, overwhelmed. She didn't know what to do.

Miguel watched her from his seat, equally unsure. Professing his love was not something new to him. This, however, was so much more than he'd ever felt before. He'd never understood what he was saying before. This time, he truly meant it. He'd never before

214

had to wait, practically unable to breathe; hoping endlessly that she returned his affection. He thought he understood women to an extent, but watching Maria pace, obviously struggling with something, he knew he didn't have a clue.

Gathering his courage, he went and put his arms around her. She leaned into him, resting her head on his chest, filling him with that deep sense of peace and calm he'd never known except with her. He stroked her hair, marveling at the way it flowed between his fingers, leading his hand down to her slender back.

Miguel's presence was so calming. In his arms, everything in a world that had been falling apart around her suddenly felt right to Maria. Here, she was safe. With her head still on his chest she whispered the words they'd both been waiting for. "I love you, Miguel."

Miguel tilted her head back and looked into her dark eyes. Her heart seemed to stop as he leaned down and their lips met. Her eyes closed and she inhaled, taking in the smell of him, horse and leather and cedar. Her arms reached around his neck and pulled him closer as his hands slid to her waist and did the same.

Chapter 16

SPRING 1740

A S THE DAYS passed, Ciro took more and more of Miguel's time, but rather than daring the world without him, Maria simply went out less. She remained hesitant to leave her father's home without her escort, and though they often went on rides through the countryside in the evenings, she grew restless. Determined to take control over her life, she decided to try something drastic.

Maria pushed the food around on her plate as Miguel and her father continued to talk business over supper. Normally, she would have tried to guide the conversation elsewhere, but tonight, her stomach was filled with butterflies. Perhaps she should have asked Miguel his opinion first.

"You've been quiet tonight," Maria's father said, and both the men looked over at her.

Too late.

"Papa," Maria said, taking a deep breath.

"Yes, *hija*?" Ciro smiled at her.

Maria swallowed and tried not to rush as she spilled her thoughts. "I have decided that since Miguel has become increasingly more involved with you and the business, and since I cannot spend the rest of my life within the walls of our *hacienda*, I would like to learn to shoot." Miguel nearly choked on his food as he gave her an incredulous look. She definitely should have spoken to him first. Her father, on the other hand, nodded thoughtfully.

"I have actually been thinking about that myself. Perhaps it would be best, though, if Miguel took you. As much as I hate to admit it, he's a better shot than me." He gave Miguel an appraising look. "We can move more of the paperwork to the evenings; I can do that on my own easily enough. I think you've got the hang of it, Miguel, don't you think?"

"Yes, Señor," Miguel answered, still trying to clear his throat. "I think I understand how it works."

"Excellent. Then it seems that in addition to your other duties, you will be teaching my daughter to shoot in the evenings as the weather permits. You two go out riding every afternoon, anyhow. I'm sure you'd rather do something more productive with that time than *abraz*—"

"Of course, Señor," Miguel hastily cut in as Maria blushed, her relief turning to embarrassment. "I'd be happy to teach Maria."

"Shooting, Miguel. Teach my daughter shooting." Ciro grinned at Miguel as Maria blushed deeper and tried to disappear into her chair.

"Of course, Señor," Miguel said, trying to cover a grin with a drink.

"Now, that brings up another thing I'd been meaning to speak to both of you about." Ciro sat back. Maria gave him a horrified look, and he chuckled. "Well, I suppose it can wait."

***

The next day, Maria paced through the house and changed her dress three times, trying to make sure she wore just the right thing. What did one wear to learn to shoot a pistol, anyway? What if it rained while they were out?

Anxiety at holding a gun again snaked its way through her thoughts, held precariously at bay by any distraction she could find. At the moment, she focused on the riddle of what had tipped off her father as to why she and Miguel had been spending so much time together. Where had his suspicion come from? How could he possibly know? They weren't really doing anything *wrong*, though perhaps a bit inappropriate for a couple who weren't yet engaged... She pulled on a pair of leather riding gloves. Would he be angry if he knew for sure? Would he approve of Miguel? How in the world did her father know? She certainly hadn't told anyone. Miguel! She tore the gloves off again and threw them on the nearest chair. Was he gossiping about her? To her *father! Oh, I'll kill him!*

When the time neared, Maria ordered the horses saddled and brought around to the front. She found a parasol in case it started to rain and then sought out Miguel, who was with her father in his study.

"Ah, it would appear that it is time for my daughter's lessons, Miguel," her father said when she appeared in the door.

"So it would." Miguel turned to her and bowed. "My lady."

"Miguel." Maria curtsied back.

"Señor, I beg your leave. I'd hate to keep such a lovely young woman waiting," Miguel said.

"Of course. Maria, have you a pistol?" Ciro looked back down at his papers.

The question took Maria completely off guard.

At the silence that followed Ciro laughed. "No, I suppose you wouldn't. Miguel, there is a box over on that shelf, the one with the inlaid ivory."

Miguel retrieved the box and brought it to Ciro's desk. Curious, Maria came over and watched Miguel open it. Inside were two beautiful matching pistols.

"They are for you, Maria, though Miguel will determine when you can have them. I'd like you to try to keep them on your person after that, though."

Maria nodded, wanting to run her fingers along the beautiful worked handles but repelled by them at the same time.

"Miguel, make sure she understands how to safely handle them as well as shoot them. Please also consider what we spoke about earlier."

"Certainly, Señor. Señorita?" Miguel offered his arm to Maria and tucked the box with the pistols under the other.

They rode north toward the strait until they came to an abandoned building with a half-fallen fence nearby. What had seemed like a good, logical idea to Maria suddenly made her ill. Bad things happened around guns. They dismounted, and Miguel tied the horses near the shack, removing the greatcoat she had given him and tossing it over his horse's saddle. Untying the box with her father's pistols, he gestured her to a small boulder several paces from the derelict fence posts.

"First, I will explain to you how these work." Miguel pulled out one of the pistols as she neared, pointing it at the ground.

"I know how they work. My father explained them to me once when I was a girl" Maria confidently picked up the other. The metal along the handle burned cold against her palm, but rather than drop it, she gripped tighter. She would do this.

"All right then, impress me." Miguel tucked her father's pistol away.

"This is the barrel where the shot comes out." She lifted the gun to show him, and he jerked back, pushing the barrel away from him.

"Lesson one: muzzle control. Don't point that thing at anything you don't want to kill."

He said it with a smile, but ice shot through her veins. She wouldn't think about it. Turning to face the fence post squarely, she continued.

"These pistols are rifled inside, which makes the shot spin as it comes out. The spin helps the pistol shoot true, though not all guns have this." Pointing to the bit above the handle, she continued. "This is the flintlock, and when the hammer is cocked all the way back and the trigger is pulled, the flint on the flintlock sparks the gunpowder in the frizzen. The resulting explosion is what shoots the ball." She smiled, hoping she'd impressed Miguel.

"Not bad, but tell me …." Miguel pulled his own pistol from within his jacket and shot at the distant post. A puff of dust erupted from the wood. He held the gun out for Maria. "Now how do you shoot?"

"I suppose you reload it … oh, don't even start with me!" She grinned and shoved at him playfully. "You'll have to tell me how."

"So, your gun is empty. You pull the hammer back halfway; this position is called 'lock.'" Miguel demonstrated as he spoke. "Then you load the powder and shot. If it is a muzzle load, like mine, you use the ramrod, here, to shove it all down the barrel, like this."

"So, lock—" she repeated his actions on her empty pistol "—and load."

"Then you must prime the flash pan, like so." He added some of the fine powder and closed the frizzen, then held out the powder to her. "Your pistol is now primed and ready. It's the same with muskets; they're just larger."

Maria copied him as he spoke. "Surely there is a better way to do this. It seems it would take far too long during a fight," Maria commented as she finished priming her pistol. Now that her pistol was ready to shoot, death held in potential in her hands, her guts clenched.

"It's been the best technology around for a hundred years. A good soldier can shoot, reload, and shoot again in fifteen seconds. Also, I keep my pistols locked and loaded whenever I go out, so all I need is to pull the cock the rest of the way back, aim, and fire."

"Pistols? As in more than one?" Maria gave him a look, careful to keep her pistol aimed at the dirt several feet away from them.

Miguel grinned and pulled the hammer of his pistol the rest of the way back. "Now, you aim your gun like so, lining the barrel up with your target, and squeeze the trigger." He aimed at the fence again and shot, once again hitting the dilapidated post squarely in the middle.

Maria nodded and stepped up beside him. She looked at the target, her hands suddenly sweaty. She could do this. She would do this.

"Full cock."

Maria raised her arm, but a trembling began in her stomach and radiated out her arms. She could do this. It was just a post. Not a man.

"Aim."

Maria took one deep breath and then another.

Miguel stepped up beside her, his hand pressed against the small of her back. It steadied her, and the trembling subsided as she focused on the pressure of his hand and ignored the rest of the world.

"Fire," he whispered.

She closed her eyes and pulled the trigger. The gun leapt from her hands. Maria's eyes flew open as the gun landed with a heavy thud several feet away and Miguel burst out laughing.

"What did I do wrong?" she asked, bewildered, as Miguel picked up the pistol.

"Reload, and I'll help you next time." Miguel grinned and handed back the pistol.

She reloaded, determined to do better this time, to be steady. Again, Miguel stepped up behind her, the warmth of his body pressed against her back, and the feel of his arms along hers distracted her for a moment. *Focus,* she chided herself. Resetting her stance, she allowed him to guide her arm with his.

"Now, you want to aim." He moved his face beside hers and spoke into her ear. "Set your sights down the barrel, there, but keep your eyes open this time and prepare for the recoil. It's not much, and you should be able to handle it if you're ready."

His hands lay strong and steady over hers, and her heart beat faster as she couldn't help but note the strength and solidity of him. *Focus,* she reprimanded herself again. This time when she shot, she hit the trees just behind the fence post. A thrill shot through her at finding the pistol still in her hands as Miguel stepped away. The apprehension that had grown in her all morning evaporated.

"I didn't drop it!" She gave him a triumphant smile, showing him the gun, and he grinned back at her joy.

"Good! Now reload and try again. This time though, gently squeeze the trigger," he said as he sat on a nearby rock. "And remember *never* to point that thing anywhere but the ground and your target."

They passed the remainder of the afternoon that way, Maria shot, reloaded, and shot again, while Miguel sat on his rock and watched, correcting her when needed. They continued until the sun began to set and the wind picked up. Maria ruefully rubbed her aching arm and shoulder muscles as they rode in companionable silence.

"What was it that my father wanted you to consider?" Maria asked.

"Hmmm? When?" Miguel asked.

"Today before we left. He asked you to consider what you had discussed?"

"That. Right." Miguel was silent for a few moments as he gathered his thoughts. "Maria, your father knows that we've grown close."

"Who told him that, I wonder?" Maria said, annoyance coloring her voice.

"Maria, everyone knows it." He shook his head. "Anyone who has ever been in love can see it. We're not exactly discreet."

Maria blushed at her naiveté and looked at her hands and the smooth leather reins she held. She felt silly she hadn't considered that possibility.

Miguel continued. "Your father is still very much in love with your mother. He misses her terribly, for all that she's been dead for seventeen years. It's amazing, really, that he never sought to fill the void she left."

Maria gave him a sharp look and he cleared his throat.

"Anyhow, your father, well, um ... he thinks it would be best, since it is obvious that we have become close, that we make public that we are courting."

"Courting?" Maria teased, enjoying his discomfort.

"Well, I'd like to court you, officially." Miguel stumbled over his words. "That is, if you want to ...."

Maria grinned. She loved ruffling him; he was always so proper around everyone else. "Well, if my *father* thinks it's a good idea, I'll just have to go along with it."

Miguel smiled back at her and reached over to squeeze her hand.

***

The wind whipped the rain into Miguel's face like so many branches, despite his hat, and he ducked his head beneath his arm, feeling sorry for his steadfast gelding who had no such protection. Ciro rode beside him as they made their way home. Miguel wasn't sure if he should curse the weather that kept him from speaking to Ciro, or thank it. He'd been hearing rumors that worried him, of Gonza, and of the Wayuu. Both topics Ciro did not like to discuss.

A large branch crashed down in front of them as they reached the gates to the *hacienda,* and Ciro cursed as Miguel fought to keep his horse from rearing. By the time the men had their horses under control, dancing around the offending branch as the trees reached menacingly toward them, the gate had been opened. Miguel resisted the urge to rush his horse through the courtyard. It was no small relief when the horses finally stepped into the shelter of the *hacienda's* stable, and Miguel slid from his gelding's back.

"Do you always choose the worst storm of the year to ride out in?" he asked Ciro as he handed a stablehand the reins.

"This? This is hardly a storm at all. Just some wind," Ciro said with a rakish grin and a slap on the back for Miguel.

"At least it's warm here." Miguel adjusted his heavy greatcoat.

"It is that." Ciro removed his own coat. "I can never decide if I want the protection my coat will give me or the relief from the heat I'd get by leaving it behind."

"And risk my powder getting wet?" Miguel shook his head as he checked his pistols. "Never."

"That's what I like about you; you know when to take risks, and when not to." Ciro gestured to the door, and they walked.

Miguel swallowed. Ciro had been pushing more and more for him to take an active role in decisions lately. It was now or never. "Speaking of risks, Gonza

226

is certainly taking one, putting so much of his wealth into just a few ships."

"Putting so much of his clients' wealth into so few ships," Ciro responded thoughtfully. "And far too many of those ships are mine. If the journey goes well, the risk will pay off well for him, but if any one of those ships goes down, he'll be a ruined man. It is utterly foolish of him."

Their conversation paused as they rushed from the stables through the storm and into the house. So far, so good. Miguel decided to press on.

"Do you think he'll blame you personally if anything happens?" Miguel asked, shaking the water from his greatcoat and passing it and his hat to the footman.

"Naturally." Ciro moved into the study and sat heavily on the couch.

The wind rattled branches against the windows as Miguel followed suit, sitting across from him. "The question then, I suppose, is what will he do, and what will we do to prevent it?"

Ciro leaned back, stretching his legs before him, but didn't respond.

"Is he still after your support for the war?" Miguel asked, braving the topic Ciro liked least. "Would that be a viable buffer, do you think? Could you convince him to take fewer risks if you agreed?"

Leaning forward, Ciro looked Miguel in the eye. "That will never be a possibility." He ran his hand through his wet hair. "That is certainly an issue, though.

I can't be seen to support the rabble rousing, but if it comes to it, I can't risk being seen to not help. If I'm deemed a traitor, Maria could lose everything I've built for her."

Miguel leaned back, loosening his damp cravat. The issue here was Gonza. He, more than anyone, pushed folks to stir up animosity about the natives. He had far too much influence that way. If there was something that could bring him down ….

"What if you lost one of your ships?" Miguel suggested.

Ciro gave him a calculating look. "Would you be willing to go down with that ship and her crew, my boy?"

Miguel shook his head. "Not sink, just ... lose. For a little while. Ships are late all the time. This one would only need to be late long enough. And if we plan for it, we should be able to get by."

"Plan for what?" Maria's voice from the doorway made them both turn.

"It's just business," Ciro said. "Nothing you need to be concerned with."

Maria entered and stood by the sideboard. Miguel always enjoyed watching her gather her courage, the way she would take a deep breath and square her shoulders. There it was—she raised her chin and turned back to her father. Miguel smiled, wondering what unexpected thing she'd come up with this time.

"I would like to be more involved in the family business, Papa." Her voice remained level and even.

Miguel silently applauded her courage, even if he disapproved. He glanced at Ciro who looked pleased.

"I have a good head for figures, and excellent penmanship, and, after all, it is a *family* business, and I think it's important that I know what is going on."

Ciro stood and hugged his daughter. "I think it is a wonderful idea. Your mother always enjoyed being involved, as well. I'm sure most of the smartest decisions we made were her ideas, anyway."

Maria beamed at her father.

"I think we're done for the day, as it is." He stepped back. "Would you see when dinner will be ready while Miguel and I change into some dry clothes?"

Maria nodded and shot Miguel a smile as she left.

"I'm not sure this is such a good idea," Miguel said cautiously as Ciro shut the door behind her. "She could get hurt. What if Gonza goes after her again?"

"We'll keep the estate secure. I'll see that Sergio does the same to Casa de la Cuesta, and she doesn't go out without you anyhow. Most of the business is administration and paperwork, anyway, and she's right that she's got a good head for that sort of thing. She'll stay safe, and you and I will manage the rough things. Besides, I have no interest in telling her she can't do something. Do you?"

Miguel stood, water still squishing in his boots. It would be nice to get into dry clothes. He shook his head. "I'm not sure it's possible to stop her once she's got the bit between her teeth, anyway."

Ciro laughed and opened the door. "You're learning."

***

Things fell into a new pattern for Maria. She spent more time each day learning how her father's business ran; their clients, their accounts, and the histories thereof. In the evening, when the rain and wind seemed unlikely to be severe, she and Miguel would ride to the broken-down shed where Maria practiced shooting, reloading, and shooting again. After a few days, Miguel added smaller targets to the fence post.

When she complained about the constant ache in her arm, shoulder, and back, Miguel introduced basic knife fighting and swordsmanship in conjunction with the use of the pistol. For safety's sake, they used a mock pistol, lathes, and short sticks for the fighting lessons. Whenever Maria began to think she could get the upper hand, Miguel would surprise her with something she hadn't thought of before. Sometimes, when he'd pinned her, he would steal a kiss on her cheek before she figured out how to break free.

"That's terribly distracting," she once said, giving him a good-natured shove after they'd broken apart.

"Then you shouldn't let yourself be distracted," he countered with a grin as she prepared to attack again.

She gave a mischievous smile. If that was how he was going to be, then she'd distract him, instead.

"You're impossible!" she exclaimed several failed attempts later.

"In what way?" he asked, taking a seat on the stone.

She rolled her eyes, reaching up to lift her windswept hair from her sweating neck. "To distract."

"Everyone can be distracted." He smiled, watching. "It's just a matter of discovering what they're susceptible to."

"And just what are you susceptible to?" Maria asked, dropping her hands to her hips. "Obviously not my wiles."

"Oh, I'm susceptible to your wiles, just not during a fight."

"So how would I beat you in a fight?" She stepped closer to him.

"A wise man never gives away his weaknesses," he said sagely.

Maria shook her head and tried to push him off the rock. He grabbed her wrist and pulled her down onto his lap instead, leaning her back.

"See, now this is a position you wouldn't want to find yourself in." He leaned toward her, his voice husky. "What are you going to do about it?"

Maria's heart pounded in her chest. "I could scream."

"I could kiss you; then who would hear?" He leaned closer, pressing against her.

She tried to keep her mind off how close his lips were to hers.

"I could grab your hair." She brought her hand to his face. "Or hit your jaw with my palm."

He gently took her wrist, then moved it firmly to her waist, his eyes glancing down to her lips as he drew her closer, whispering into her ear. "Now what would you do?"

She tried pulling back her head so she could think about something beyond the texture of his scruff against her cheek or the deep warmth that filled her, but his hand on the base of her neck kept her from doing so. Perhaps she could kick him somehow …? As she twisted to bring her foot around, she overcorrected, jerking her head forward and bashing his nose with her forehead.

Immediately, his grip on her loosened as he reached for his face and she toppled onto the ground. He reached for her, losing his balance as she landed on his feet, and fell in a heap beside her with a grunt.

"Did I hurt you?" Maria immediately tried to sit up, but her skirts were tangled around her legs. Scowling, she pulled them around to free her feet, as Miguel sat up.

"I'm so sorry!" Miguel said as he sat up, his voice choked. "Are you all right? I can't believe I dropped you—"

Maria turned back to him, inadvertently hitting his face with her elbow. This time, Miguel let himself fall to his back, one hand pinching his bleeding nose and the other flung above his head.

"You win. I surrender!" he called out, laughing.

Maria gathered her skirts and knelt beside him, poking him in the side. "Ha, I finally bested you."

"Yes, you finally did. Serves me right, too. I was not expecting that."

Dusting off her skirt with mock arrogance, she looked down at him. "Well, I'd hate to bore you."

"I doubt that is even possible. Though I might be a bit dull while I lie here until my nose stops bleeding and I can gather the broken pieces of my pride." He exhaled and closed his eyes.

"Don't worry, I won't tell anyone. We'll say the horse did it."

"I'm not sure that would be all that much better."

Maria stood as another burst of wind blew across the field. She reached down to help Miguel stand. "We'd better head back; it'll rain soon."

***

The length of their practice sessions grew shorter as they spent more time talking, walking, or simply riding at a leisurely pace. As the rain became more frequent and heavy, Maria spent the afternoons with Nana. They worked on the best ways to alter her dresses to allow for a knife or two and a pistol to be carried on her person, along with additional small pockets for powder and shot, just in case. Nana pretended to be upset at the impropriety of Maria carrying weapons, but when it failed to ruffle her young mistress, Nana took to fretting about the dresses.

Despite all the grumbling, Maria could tell Nana was both pleased and proud of her for learning to defend herself.

Chapter 17

THE DAY OF BETANIA'S wedding to Benito Garcia Arce dawned bright and clear. Midway between the first and second rainy seasons meant the rain would be minimal. Or at least, that was the hope in July. Maria spent most of the morning helping her father and Miguel get through their work quickly so that they would not be behind the next day. Around noon, Maria returned to her rooms to get dressed, hoping that the men wouldn't wait too long before getting ready themselves.

Maria entered her room to see a dress already laid out on her bed. She wrinkled her nose at it. It was the red dress she had worn to the masked ball what seemed like an eternity ago.

"Why is this old thing out, Nana?" Maria asked, pulling at the pins that held up her hair. She didn't want to think of the dark stains that had covered the skirt the last time she'd seen it. "Surely I have something better."

"That 'old thing' was new the last time you wore it, *chica*," Nana said, backing into the room, her arms full of petticoats. "The *only* time you wore it, I might add."

"But everyone has seen me in it already. I ought to wear something else." Maria picked up the dress, holding it at arm's length as she returned it to the wardrobe.

"I think not." Nana took the dress from Maria and laid it back on the bed. "It compliments your features exquisitely."

"I don't want to wear it." Maria sighed, knowing that her ploy had failed.

"And why is that?" Nana gave Maria a challenging look.

"It … makes my skin crawl to even look at it," Maria admitted, shuddering.

"See? It wasn't so hard to tell old Nana the truth, now was it," Nana said simply, returning the dress to the wardrobe. "Start getting changed. I'll bring out another one."

Maria removed her dress and changed her petticoats, looking with disgust at the corset waiting for her. She stalled as long as she could before putting it on and having Nana cinch it for her. Despite the modifications they'd made to it to allow her to breathe should she need to run, or maneuver should she need to fight, it was still tight, confining, and uncomfortable. Maria hated the thing. Nana simply chuckled as she helped lace it up.

"It's things like this that tempt me to simply wear a man's clothes," Maria grumbled as Nana yanked on the strings.

"I'm not sure how well you'd be able to pull that off. Your bosom is much too large," Nana stated as Maria twisted her shoulders and hips, readjusting the set of the corset.

Maria looked back at her old nursemaid, appraising the woman's sagging breasts.

"You can have mine, but I'm afraid I don't want yours in return," Maria said with a final tug at her shift.

"I'm afraid I'm content with mine. You'll just have to give yours to someone else." Nana lifted the new gown, red and black brocade with golden lace, over Maria's head. It settled gently over her underpinnings, and Nana started on the laces.

Nana turned Maria around to make sure nothing had been forgotten. Satisfied, Nana opened the door to the hall to allow the air to pass through the hot room. Maria turned to her mirror and started on her hair.

"Hair is as annoying as breasts," she said, as Nana took over Maria's hair.

"I've worked hard to start ridding myself of that, too, but it just keeps coming back," Nana whispered conspiratorially to Maria.

Maria laughed at the thought of Nana, who had long silver tresses, bald.

"I'll give them to Miguel, then," Maria said.

"I'm sure he'd appreciate that," Nana chortled.

"Give me what?" Miguel said from the doorway. Maria spun so fast she knocked her powder to the floor. "How long have you been there?!"

"Sorry, I was passing in the hall when I heard my name," he said at the same time, stepping back.

"Her breasts," Nana said over them both.

"Excuse me?" Miguel asked, looking incredulously at Nana while Maria blushed and turned away from them both, appalled to realize that she still faced him by way of the mirror.

"She has decided to give you her breasts in exchange for your clothes," Nana said in a most somber voice.

"Nana!" Maria cried, shocked and too embarrassed to face Miguel in the doorway or the mirror. She turned instead toward the window, covering her face with her hands.

"Um …." Miguel stood there speechless for a moment, and then in a choked voice said, "I'll, just, um, be on my way. Sorry to disturb you, Señorita." Maria watched through the mirror as he bowed to her back, looking at the floor the whole time, and hurried on his way.

"That was completely uncalled for!" Maria rushed to shut the door. No cooling breeze was worth enduring that.

"It was nothing but the truth." Nana shrugged as she finished Maria's hair and tied on her mother's necklace.

When she was ready, Maria peeked cautiously out her door, relieved to find only an empty hall. With one last glare at Nana, she stepped out, throwing her shoulders back and putting up her chin, determined to pretend nothing had happened the next time she saw Miguel. Maybe he would forget about it.

She fiddled with the knickknacks in the entryway as she waited for the men to appear, working herself up to remain calm. Her father appeared first. She smiled at him and set her hand in his offered arm. She gripped his sleeve as they approached the waiting coach. Maria clamped down on the nerves that threatened to upset her hard-won calm. It was only a coach. She had done other, harder things. She could do this, too.

"Where is Miguel?" she asked, careful to sound unconcerned as her father helped her in.

"On his way, I imagine." Ciro climbed in after her and took a seat beside her. His steadying presence did almost as much to calm her as Miguel's would have.

"I do hope he doesn't keep us waiting too long," she said, proud of her voice for remaining level.

Miguel appeared shortly thereafter, apologizing for holding them up as he climbed in and sat across from father and daughter.

"Nothing to worry yourself about, *muchacho*," Ciro replied.

Maria watched Miguel as he kept his eyes averted from her, looking out the window, at the floor, the ceiling, or Ciro. When he did look her way, their eyes locked for a moment. She quickly looked down, blushing fiercely and fidgeting under his intense gaze. Finally, she looked out the window, afraid to meet his eyes again.

The loaded silence in the coach lengthened. After a time, Maria chanced another look at Miguel, only to be caught up in his eyes again. This time, when she broke contact, she cast a discreet look at her father and saw him leaning back, watching them with a grin.

I hope you're entertained, she thought sarcastically. She sighed and looked at her hands as she fiddled with her gloves. Her sigh seemed to break the spell, and the men began to chat. She ignored it, preferring to watch the passing scenery.

When they reached the Casa de la Cuesta, Ciro left them, claiming he had some people to speak to. Miguel took Maria's arm, maintaining propriety with an exacting stubbornness. Maria could feel him next to her, as if lightning were jumping between them, his touch like fire on her arm. When she looked up at the front of the de la Cuesta mansion, Miguel's presence faded somewhat under a pang of nostalgia.

"I can hardly believe it has been so long since I've been here." Maria took in the grand plantation home with its sweeping arches and manicured foliage.

Miguel nodded. "Nearly six months."

They walked on until they reached a large group of wedding guests, where they were obliged to exchange greetings and courtesies. When they had finally made their way through the gauntlet, Miguel led Maria to a bench.

"What are weddings like on the other side of the world?" Maria asked as she sat, moving aside her skirt to make room for Miguel.

"I've seen many weddings in dozens of places. They all have their own unique customs, but many things are the same. For instance, most of them have some sort of tradition that indicates which unmarried man or woman will be next to marry," Miguel said after taking a measured look at Maria.

"We have something like that, too. The bride gives gifts to all the guests. The single women get pins or brooches"—Maria showed Miguel hers, a sweeping, worked silver vine with three dark enameled roses to one side—"which they wear upside down. If I were to lose it during the festivities, then I would supposedly be the next in line to marry."

"I see. What about an exchange of gifts between the bride and groom?"

"The groom gives either the bride or her father thirteen gold coins, called *arras*. This shows that he can support her."

"And when do they do that?"

"They can do it either as part of the ceremony or beforehand. It doesn't really matter." Maria noticed a stir in the guests and stood up and grinned. "It would appear to be time to start the procession."

Miguel and Maria turned the same direction as the rest of the guests just in time to see Betania emerge. Her black silk dress looked amazing on her, and Maria couldn't help the small sigh that escaped her. An intricate black lace veil covered her face, matching the black lace trim on her dress. Betania's father, Don Sergio Díaz Montejo, Señor de la Cuesta, escorted her, walking along proudly enough to put a rooster to shame.

Maria reached for Miguel's hand as the guests cheered among a buzz of comments on the beauty of the bride and her dress. Don Sergio and his eldest daughter made their way out the front door to the waiting carriage. Following them were Doña Olivia and Elisa, resplendent in their dresses. When Elisa saw Miguel and Maria standing together she slowed a little and gave them an icy glare, before hurrying after her family.

One by one, the wedding guests climbed back into their carriages or walked beside the bride's for the procession to the chapel. Don Ciro appeared through the crowd just as their coach did, and the three of them climbed in, making room for an elderly couple whom Ciro had invited to join them. They spoke of business and politics and the tensions with the Wayuu, speculating on the likelihood of yet another rebellion. The elderly woman staunchly insisted that it would never happen again, not after the last one with their two thousand warriors, and even if it did, it would never come close to that number again, that the natives should simply be content with what the Spanish gave them. Her husband agreed with her with an air of weariness from trying to explain the reality of the situation to her. Don Ciro tried to explain why it not only could, but

242

likely would happen again, if certain things didn't change. Miguel paid careful attention to the entire exchange, but Maria let her gaze and her mind wander.

For a time, she allowed her eyes to travel over Miguel's well-fitting clothes. They were a far cry from what he had worn the first time they'd met. These clothes were new, newer than even what he had worn to the masked ball, and rather finer, too. Even the gleaming boots were new, though already broken in. For once, he wasn't wearing the greatcoat she'd given him. The thought of how badly it would have clashed made her smile. The coat he'd had the day they met had been so weathered that the initial color was only hinted at, whereas this dress coat, tailored in the latest fashion, matched his pants and vest.

Despite the fancy appearance, she knew that under the coat were at least two half-cocked pistols and three or more knives secreted about his body. He was taller now, at nearly twenty years old, than he had been a year and a half ago. She admired how nicely he'd filled out in his chest and shoulders. The thought of his body made her blush again, and she looked up to see him watching her. She blushed even harder and looked out the window. She loved the way he looked at her but hated how shy she was about it in public.

They arrived at the chapel and filed in. Benito was escorted down the aisle by his mother, followed by Betania with her father. She looked radiant and so full of joy under her black veil that Maria couldn't help smiling herself. She watched rather longingly as the priest performed the ceremony, the coins were exchanged, and a rosary was wrapped around the couple.

The entire company followed the new couple back to the Casa de la Cuesta for the wedding festivities. Betania and Benito danced the wedding dance, *Seguidillas Manchegas*, and then circled the room to visit with the guests.

"Oh, Maria, I can't believe how happy I am!" Betania exclaimed once the couple reached them. "It seems like only yesterday we announced our engagement. I hope you find as much happiness!"

"I don't know." Maria laughed. "I think you're going to use up the world's supply of happiness tonight, if you don't burst from it first!"

Betania leaned to her, "Honestly, though, I hope you marry Miguel. He seems like such a good man for you."

"What about your sister?" Maria asked. "Wouldn't you rather see him with her?"

"Absolutely not." Betania's face turned serious. "She would ruin him. She's been all in a flurry since the announcement about you. She's changed. She's so … vicious now. She told me she was the one who ordered the servants to leave you alone at the ball. It's probably best that you stay away from her."

"Don't worry about that." Maria waved her back. "Now, let's not talk of such dreary things! This is your wedding! *Felicitaciones!* Go, enjoy yourselves!"

Betania smiled her appreciation and took Benito's arm, and they moved on. Miguel pulled Maria out to dance as the next song began.

"Why the long face?" Miguel asked as they danced.

"It's just that ...." Maria began, stumbling over her words as she tried to sort through her emotions. "Elisa. Do you suppose she knew what would happen that night?"

"I seriously doubt it. How could she have known unless she was a conspirator? She was just being mean-spirited. Probably thought no further than to inconvenience and annoy you."

"Did you know it was her?" Maria looked up into his lovely green eyes.

"Of course. Your father spoke with Don Sergio immediately, and naturally, they spoke with the staff. Don't worry about it, *mi morena*. We took care of it." He smiled at her and she felt herself relax. Now was not the time to fret about Elisa anyhow. Tonight was to be enjoyed.

They danced together throughout the night, and occasionally with other partners, though each never let the other out of sight. They also kept a wary eye on Elisa and found excuses to move about the room, keeping as much distance from her as they politely could.

As the evening wore on, Maria found Miguel and pulled him out to a balcony to take a break from the heat and noise. She led him to the bannister and leaned over it, watching the gardens in the moonlight. She wanted to talk to him, just to listen to his voice, but couldn't find the words. The evening was too perfect for words.

Figures moved through the gardens below, as they had the last time she'd been on this balcony. Turning to ask Miguel if he would walk with her down there, she found him watching her, a crimson flower in his hand. Her mind blanked, fixated on the daring he'd shown to pick one of Doña Olivia's flowers from her planter, as he reached toward her, tucking the flower behind her ear.

Her breath caught as his hand trailed down her jaw then tilted her head up. Maria's world fell away as he kissed her tenderly in the moonlight. She melted into his arms, and he pulled away before she was ready for it to end. She smiled up at him, holding his hand on her neck.

"Let's take a walk." She gestured toward the gardens, her voice soft.

"All right," he said in a husky voice, allowing her to lead him down off the balcony. They walked across the moonlit lawn arm in arm.

"That night, at the ball," she said as they ambled down the path, "I stood on the balcony and watched couples walking down here. They seemed so oblivious to the rest of the world. I wondered if I would ever do the same with the man I love."

"And here you are," he said.

"And here you are." She squeezed his arm.

They wound their way along the paths lined with ornamental hedges and flowers, and the occasional tall roble with its wide leaves. The heavy scent of the flowers—orchids, roses, hibiscus, and others she couldn't name—mingled with the humid air. They walked aimlessly until coming to a stop before a secluded bench a little way from the main path. They sat down, and Maria leaned back against the armrest, looking at the stars.

"Why is it that you were always following me?" she asked.

"You really never figured it out?" Miguel asked, a laugh in his voice.

"I have had my suspicions, but I want to hear what you'll say," Maria said, her gaze still tracing the stars.

"Your father hired me to be your bodyguard. We called it being his 'assistant' because I was assisting him with ensuring your safety. That, and he didn't think you'd take kindly to having a stranger following you everywhere."

"So all those times you appeared, insisting that I go one way and not the other …?" She looked over at him.

"For one reason or another, I feared for your safety."

"And now?"

"Now? I am your father's business partner in fact, but I'll always be your bodyguard." He looked down to meet her eyes. "Does that bother you, Maria?"

"No," Maria said, rather surprised as she realized it really didn't. Miguel nodded and Maria returned to her celestial contemplation.

Miguel watched her for a time, thinking how beautiful she was, how charmed he was by her wit. It amazed him how he strove to be on his best behavior when she was around. A right gentleman he was turning into. His old chums from the sea and the ports around the world would hardly recognize him now. He fingered the silver brooch in his pocket that he had deftly removed from Maria's shoulder when they'd kissed, certain she hadn't noticed. Steeling his nerves, Miguel took a deep breath.

"Your pin is gone," he said.

"Huh?" Maria asked, absent-mindedly.

"Your brooch. The one you told me about earlier. It's gone." He said, touched her shoulder where the brooch had been.

She looked down at her dress and touched the bare cloth. "So it is." She smiled up at Miguel through her eyelashes.

Miguel took another moment to swallow. His mouth had gone dry and butterflies fluttered in his stomach. He took both of her hands in his and slid to the ground, kneeling before her. She looked down at him skeptically as he placed her brooch in her hands.

"What's this?" She looked at the brooch, then at him.

"Maria Álvarez Cordova, would you do me the honor of being my wife?" Miguel looked into her dark eyes. The silence that followed seemed to stretch through eternity.

"Miguel, I ... I don't know what to say ...."

"Why not? If you don't want to marry me, just say so." Miguel stood, pulling Maria up to stand next to him, worry that he'd terribly misjudged things gnawing at him.

"No, it's not that. I mean, I *do* want to. Marry you, that is, but ...." Maria turned from him, pulling his arms around her.

He held her tight to him. "But what?" he asked gently.

"I'd be so happy with you, Miguel, but, I don't deserve it. I'm a terrible person."

"Whatever do you mean? I think you're a wonderful, amazing woman who could conquer the world if she wanted."

"No, I'm not." She paused, the tension in her body speaking of her uncertainty. "Miguel, I've killed a man," she whispered, pulling a little away from him.

Miguel let out a breath of relief, unsure what to say. Of course he knew she'd killed that man in the carriage. How could he not?

She turned in his arms to face him. "Could you ever forgive me for such a thing?"

"I could forgive you anything, *mi morena*. I love you." Miguel caressed her face. When she looked away in shame, he pulled her back to her seat on the bench.

"Why don't you tell me what happened," he asked gently.

"I killed him, Miguel. The man in the carriage, the night you rescued me. He had the pistol, and it was pointed right at me, but then he was distracted, and I tried to grab the gun from him ...." Maria choked up and tears fell down her cheeks. "I must've hit my head somehow, because the next thing I knew, I was on the floor, and all I could think was that he was going to kill me, so I kicked him as hard as I could. He dropped the gun and I picked it up. And then I ... I shot him in the face. There was so much blood ...."

Maria started sobbing. Feeling helpless, Miguel wrapped her in his arms, letting her cry into his shoulder. He stroked her hair and told her everything would be all right until her sobs quieted.

"*Mi querida*, there is no shame in protecting yourself or the ones you love. I killed at least one man that night as well, possibly all three of them." He swallowed, allowing himself to feel for a moment the regret he'd carried for so long. Then he admitted something he'd never said out loud. "And they were not my first."

Maria pulled back and shook her head. "But his life—it's over. What about the people who cared about *him*? He was a person. What if somebody loved him? What if he had a wife and children? I took him away from them. He had parents at some point; somebody raised him. He had hopes and dreams."

"Maria, honey, you can't think of it like that, or it will consume you." Miguel tilted her head up gently and searched her eyes. "You have all those things, too. What right does anyone have to take that from you? He *chose* to be where he was, and he *knew* it might cost him his life. You did the right thing, the only thing, and you shouldn't be ashamed of it."

"I just don't know." She looked back up to the stars.

Miguel stood and offered her his hand. This was not how he'd imagined this evening would go, but when had his life since finding Maria ever gone the way he expected? "Come, let's get back before we're missed. Your father might start to worry."

Maria sent him a grateful smile and took his hand. They started back, walking arm in arm while Maria fiddled with the brooch Miguel had returned to her, safely in her pocket.

They were only a few feet from the main path when a loud *thwack* made Maria jump. Miguel collapsed beside her. She spun around to see a large, familiar man lumbering toward her. Stunned, she tried to take a step back but tripped and fell, her legs tangling in her skirts as she tried to regain her footing.

"'Ello, pretty li'l thing," he sneered as he loomed over her.

Then, from the shadows, Miguel jumped on him, a knife gleaming in his hand. Maria quickly untangled herself and stood, the world around her spinning as the

251

thug punched Miguel square in the jaw. He seemed to drop to the ground in slow motion.

Maria tried to go to him, but her feet were like lead weights buried in the ground. The man leaned over Miguel, wrangling the knife away and pressing it to his throat. Maria's breath came in short gasps, unable to get enough oxygen to make a sound. Everything in her screamed to do something, anything. But this man had taken down Miguel; what could she possibly do to him?

"Now tha' wasna too smart, boy. I'da let ye live if ye'd had the sense to stay down." The thug leaned closer to Miguel's face. "But sadly, for ye an' yer lady, any'ow, I'm going ter kill ye."

As the thug spoke and Miguel struggled, the world shifted beneath Maria's feet. Suddenly, everything was clear. He was just another target. She reached her hand slowly into the hidden pocket of her dress, hoping the thug wouldn't notice.

"Then, once yer good an' dead I'll take tha' chi' of a girl righ' 'ere, next ter yer still-warm corpse—"

Click.

The thug jerked his head to look at Maria but didn't get to say anything more as the powder exploded in the flintlock pistol. He fell to the ground with a satisfying thud.

Miguel looked up at her over the sudden dead-weight of the man, the smoke swirling around her face as she kept the gun trained squarely on the attacker.

Aura of Dawn

Miguel pushed him off with a grunt, pain exploding through his vision as he tried to stand. Gingerly, he picked himself up as the man on the ground stirred. A wordless fury washed over him, and he kicked the man viciously in the gut. For the moment, the pain that shot through his leg was worth the satisfaction. He turned to Maria, standing square as he'd taught her, her dark eyes fixed on their target. A mixture of pride and awe tugged a small smile onto his face as he limped to her. He reached down her arm to take the pistol from her, her finger still squeezing the trigger.

As soon as he touched the gun, she stirred, drawing the pistol back towards her. He watched silently, his head swimming, as she moved to reload the pistol.

"Take mine," he said as she fumbled in her pocket for shot. "I'll trade you back later."

She took his gun, checked the mechanisms, and set it to the holster in her skirt. When she finished, she looked at Miguel, her eyes filled with a cold calmness. "There is no shame in protecting the ones I love," she said, a small tremor belying the courageous words. "You are hurt; let's get you back to the house."

"Not as bad as it looks." He looked down at his blood-spattered clothes, then grinned wryly. "Least your dress is too dark to notice the blood."

"I seem to have bad luck with red dresses," she responded, shaking out her skirts.

"Is because," Miguel said slowly, struggling to find the words in Castilian, "they're too beautiful on you to resist allure." He limped forward, stumbling and grabbing a tree for support as his left knee gave out. Shaking her head, Maria put her arm around his waist, and he settled his left arm over her shoulder. Slowly, they hobbled forward.

"What does it take to get rid of you?" a cold voice said, and Miguel snapped up his head, his vision blurring at the pain of the sudden movement. He sagged, losing his balance, and for a moment feared he'd pull Maria down with him.

"I know you," Maria said, fear and anger clear in her voice.

The man's laugh sent a chill down Miguel's spine as his vision cleared and he steadied himself.

"Gonza." Miguel spat out the name, attempting to assess the situation through the cloud that lay over his brain.

"Aren't you two just adorable." Gonza stood, his pose relaxed as he talked, but there was something off about his movements that raised alarms in Miguel's fuzzy mind. "Two little lovebirds sitting in a bush, perfect for the taking."

Gun. Miguel closed his eyes for a moment as the world tried to spin sideways.

"I'd have rather had you alive, but I'm just as happy crushing Álvarez this way. And believe me, he will be crushed."

Miguel opened his eyes to find Gonza closer. Alarms went off in his mind, a cacophony of English and Castilian too jumbled to wrap his tongue around.

254

His eyes focused enough to see his Sharpe 8-inch flintlock at the end of his left arm. His delicate, feminine arm …? His mind struggled to resolve the inconsistency. *Maybe that* was *my blood* …. He wanted to look down and check his shirt for blood, but he fought the urge. He needed to focus. Someone was speaking.

Shoot him. Miguel squeezed the trigger, but the woman's arm didn't respond. Maybe it wasn't his left arm? Why would he shoot left-handed anyway?

Gonza moved, his arm reaching for something in his jacket.

Shoot! The gun before him trembled, wavering. Dropping. He should steady it.

Gonza sneered, stepping forward, and pulled out his own pistol.

With all the speed of a bucket of tar on a cold day, Miguel brought his right hand up to steady his mismatched left arm, laying his hand over hers. A heartbeat passed, and his left arm still didn't shoot.

Gonza's barrel cleared the holster, his teeth glinting in the bright moonlight like a demon's.

With a growl, Miguel jerked the gun to the right just enough and squeezed the trigger. The concussion filled his ears and eyes with an all-consuming white light, but he held himself as stone, unmovable, as the sound bounced around his skull.

Then he was on the ground.

Chapter 18

MARIA FOLLOWED silently behind José, who carried the semi-conscious Miguel. She'd traded out the second spent pistol of the night for another of Miguel's almost as soon as he'd fallen. Gonza had crumpled silently to the ground before them, clutching his wounded gut, and Maria hadn't given him a second look. When José appeared out of the darkness, she'd nearly shot him, too, before recognizing the de la Cuesta livery.

A few people had run to them, offering to help, but José had stopped them from coming close, urging them on with jokes about his friends having too much to drink. The three of them slipped in through one of the servant's kitchens and into a nearby room, where Miguel was tended and Maria sent someone to collect the thug and Gonza.

A part of her was surprised the staff hadn't gone running off for one of the family, or patched Miguel up quickly and shuffled them off for more "proper" care, but rather treated him like one of their own. Not that she minded; she enjoyed the earthy hospitality.

Maria washed her face and hands, watching the way the blood swirled and diffused in the water. She would *not* think of how it had gotten on her face. She refused to look at her dress. Then she sat near Miguel, trying to stay out of the way, calm, quiet, and in control of her senses.

She watched the servants tend Miguel as though he was one of them. They spoke with her without the usual formality that they used for their employers and higher-ups. Of course, now that she thought about it, it seemed they had always been more personable with her than other people. She had always taken it in stride and always treated them in kind, thinking it was just the way things were.

Something was different about the world that Maria couldn't place her finger on, as though she was seeing through new eyes. Something in her had died tonight; something monumental had shifted. She felt changed, transformed in a way. Disconnected from her world or her body.

As though to deny the thought, a pain in the palm of her hand pushed through her mental haze. She looked down and saw her hand was clenched in a fist. Opening it, she found the silver brooch Miguel had given her earlier, leaving a red mark across her skin. She turned it in her hand for a minute, watching Miguel absently. Could she accept this? She loved Miguel, but marrying him...? She'd never made such a large decision on her own before. Perhaps her father could give her advice.

A petite but stern-looking woman worked over Miguel, cleaning and binding his wounds on his chest, and he began to stir. A trail of dark hair ran down his belly, but Maria found herself too distracted at the moment to be embarrassed about seeing it.

"He should be all right, I think," the woman said, pulling his shirt back down. "Assuming he stays hydrated and rests. He's to stay down for at least a week. Longer, if he remains dizzy or his mind is clouded. His knee will take time to heal, and the knife wound on his ribs should heal well so long as it is not allowed to fester."

Maria nodded, and the woman looked her over with a critical eye. "You are certain you are not wounded?"

"I am uninjured, thank you," Maria said with a dismissive gesture, dropping the brooch into her pocket as she moved to sit beside Miguel.

The healer gave her a tight look. "Well, see to it that you don't disturb him. It is critical that he rests now."

"Of course," Maria said demurely, and the woman left.

As she sat in the chair beside the bed, he opened his eyes and gave her a groggy smile.

"I'm afraid I left your knife behind." She took his hand.

"Don't worry about it," he said slowly but clearly, as he tried to sit up.

She gently pushed him back into the pillow. "You need to rest," she said gently, and he relaxed into the bed. "How are you feeling?"

"Like ...." Miguel trailed off for a moment, and Maria held her breath. "Like I've been kicked in the head by a horse who then sat on me. My head hurts when I try to sit up, but I'll be fine. It's not anything I haven't experienced before," he said with a little shrug.

Maria nodded, relieved. His broken speech before he'd passed out had scared her almost as much as the attack. "You should rest here." Now that she felt he would be all right, her mind raced, setting in order the things that would need to be done. She had handled the immediate crisis.

Next, she would need to tell her father. And Sergio; this was his home after all. No doubt they would be together. Maria stood, certain of what she needed to do.

"Where are you going?" He tried to get up when she stood.

She pushed him gently back down, and again he complied, this time with a pained groan as he lay back. "I am going to find Don Álvarez and make him aware of what has happened. Stay here. I will return."

She had figured this out on her own; surely she could make her own decision on Miguel. Maria ran her fingers over the worked silver and roses of the brooch, smiling. As she walked out the door she pinned it back onto her shoulder, right-side up.

As she neared the more occupied portion of the house, she pulled a servant aside.

"Where is my father?" she asked, a serious tone in her voice that she'd never heard from her own mouth.

"In Don Sergio's study, Señorita, but they are talking business and do not wish to be disturbed," he said with a note of anxiety.

"I won't tell anyone you told me," she said with a smile and changed her course to Don Sergio's study. As she walked, memories of the times she and the other girls had snuck in to see what was there flitted before her. Naturally, Elisa had insisted they do it, Betania urged them to not, Selena had simply followed along, and Maria had planned the whole thing. The large wooden door that had always seemed imposing and forbidden stood before her. Pausing a moment, she checked her appearance in the mirror, scolding herself for not doing so earlier.

The woman looking back at her from the mirror felt different somehow from who she'd been just a few hours before, her dark eyes more intense. The subtle light of the candelabras in the hall cast gentle shadows across her dark red and black dress, the gold lace trim cascading from the edging. Even her hair, though slightly mussed, hardly looked amiss. How could she have had her life threatened twice within the last hour and still look no more worse for wear than if she'd been dancing?

Squaring her shoulders and raising her chin, she looked again to the forbidden door. But it was just a door. Not bothering to knock, she simply opened the door and walked in. The half a dozen or so men in the

260

room looked up at her when she entered, their conversation immediately muted. She stood her ground and locked eyes with her father.

"I am sorry to disturb you Dons, but I must speak with my father," she said firmly, no tremor of fear or uncertainty in her chest.

"Señoritas. They think they own the world when they reach that age," one of the men joked and the rest chuckled. Don Ciro, however, did not, and the others sobered when he rose.

"I believe I will speak with my daughter. Excuse me." He gestured her back toward the hall.

"Actually, Papa, you may want Señor de la Cuesta to hear what I have to tell you. It rather concerns him, too." She stood firmly in her place.

Sergio Díaz sat in his overstuffed chair, his cheeks and nose a little more red than normal. He looked from father to daughter, his look transforming from amused annoyance at the interruption to the grudging respect he had always given her father. Now it was directed at her.

She held her hands still, though they wanted to fidget under the scrutiny, and took a deep, satisfying breath.

"Dons," Sergio said with a sudden briskness. "It has been a lovely evening, but it would appear that Don Álvarez and I have some pressing private business to attend to. If you would excuse us, please make yourselves at home with the guests and enjoy the rest of the evening's festivities." Don Sergio bowed politely and gestured the men to the open door.

Once all the guests were out of the room and the door firmly shut, Don Sergio turned to the other two in the room. "Ciro, what is going on?" he asked, almost daring enough to be angry with him.

Ciro looked at Maria. "You're the one with something to say."

"You are aware, I'm sure, of my abduction last January from your plantation, Señor de la Cuesta?" She was more curt with him than perhaps she ought to have been. But she found herself fighting a sudden anger at everything that had happened.

"Certainly, and a shameful thing it was, too. Ciro and I have already discussed the implications of it on our businesses and our relationship."

Maria nodded, irritated that the effect on her had not been mentioned. "Papa, I think it prudent for you to know that there was another attack on me tonight."

"What! Here?" Sergio cried out.

Ciro ignored him. "What happened?"

"Miguel and I were walking in the gardens and were attacked. A man, I think it was one from the group before but no one I recognized from here. He came at us from behind and knocked Miguel to the ground. They fought, and the man got the better of Miguel, so I shot him."

"What? You shot your own bodyguard?" Sergio cried out in horror.

"No, I shot the attacker," she said flatly.

"How is Miguel? How are you?" Ciro asked calmly, his eyes dropping to her shoulder, then back to her face.

"He is resting. The healer said that with rest and time, he should recover."

"I'm glad to hear it." Ciro turned to Sergio. "Señor, that is twice now, within six months, that there has been an attempt on my household. Both times on your plantation."

"Just what are you implying?" Sergio folded his arms defensively over his chest.

"At the very least, my friend, that your house needs further looking to."

Sergio stood at the accusation and glared at Ciro a moment before turning to pour another glass from the decanter, muttering about his daughter's wedding and his wife's wrath.

"Papa." Maria put her hand on his arm. He turned back to her and she dropped her voice so that Sergio would not overhear. "That wasn't all. After I disabled the first man, another came. This one was well dressed, and I'm sure I've seen him before. I … I thought I heard Miguel say 'Gonza'."

Her father's muscles bulged under her hand as he clenched his fist.

"But isn't he a business partner of yours? What would he want with me?"

"We've got to send people to find him, and quickly." Ciro started for the door.

"I already have, Papa."

Ciro gave a curt nod of approval to Maria, and then addressed Sergio. "Until he is found and we get to the bottom of what has happened, this place can no longer be considered a safe house. Sergio, we will need to withdraw for a time …." Ciro trailed off, and both the men looked at Maria.

"What do you need from me?" Maria asked.

"For now, take the carriage and get Miguel home quickly. Have the servants secure the *hacienda*. I will come on horseback when I can. Do not worry, *hija*. They will not make another attempt on us tonight."

Maria opened the door, certain she could accomplish the requested task, but paused as Ciro continued.

"Oh, and Maria? Tell Miguel that he has my blessing." Ciro turned back to Sergio, and they were scheming before Maria had even closed the door.

Warmth filled Maria as she made her way back to the servants' quarters. Things suddenly seemed less dire than they had half an hour before. She ordered the coach brought around and sat beside Miguel's bed, watching him sleep. He looked so peaceful in the flickering lamplight. Smiling, she reached out and moved aside a lock of the dark, silky hair which had fallen into his face.

His green eyes opened and he smiled up at her. "*Mi morena*," he murmured.

"Can you get up? It's time to go home."

"I think so, if you give me a hand?" He grunted as he pulled himself up with Maria's support. Once up, he

264

wavered, and she paused, waiting for the dizziness to subside.

"Your carriage is waiting just outside," one of the servants rushed up to tell them.

"*Gracias.*" She nodded. He bowed slightly, wringing his hands, and waited to escort them out. Miguel tried to wave off Maria as they walked, but she glared at him until he allowed her to help.

While Miguel climbed into the coach, Maria checked that the driver was one of her father's men before following suit. As she stepped in, she hesitated a moment over whether to sit beside or across from Miguel. She settled herself beside him and rested his head on her shoulder.

The carriage leapt forward at a brisk pace, and though the roads on the de la Cuesta plantation were kept maintained and relatively smooth, it was still a rough ride. She held on tightly to Miguel so that he could relax and not have to focus on keeping his seat. Though he didn't make any sound, his face paled further with each jolt, and his jaw clenched tight against the pain. She had so much she wanted to say to him, needed to say to him, but she couldn't find the words to start. After a time, Miguel heaved a sigh and sat up, pulling out of Maria's arms.

"I think I'm all right now," he said, his voice thin.

She nodded despite her misgivings and moved to the seat opposite him so that they could face each other while they spoke.

"That was one of the same men from before," she blurted out. "I didn't get a terribly clear look at his face, but he looked and sounded very familiar."

"I imagine it was." Miguel nodded, his eyes tight. "I don't trust my memory at the moment, but were there two, or did I just hit my head really hard?"

"Both. You called the second man Gonza."

Miguel dropped his face into his hands with a groan. "I hoped I'd imagined that one."

"On some level, I've always known my father has enemies." Maria gave a sharp laugh. "Though it's only been real to me the last few months. I can't understand this man's hatred, though. Why would he hold such a grudge against my father?"

"I don't know. Don Ciro shares much with me about his current business, but he does not share about his past. I'm no law expert, but as far as I can tell, everything he does now is legitimate and legal. That, in and of itself, might be part of the issue, though."

"That sounds like him. He always refuses to talk about my mother, too. I wonder if that has anything to do with this Gonza person."

"I don't know. It might."

They lapsed back into silence.

Miguel looked over the woman across from him as his brain struggled to remain on one topic for more than a few seconds. She was very beautiful. He'd thought that from the beginning. More than that, though, he loved the person within. He loved making her smile,

266

hearing her laugh, the way she said things, and even more, the things she said.

Maria had turned her head to the window, watching the dark landscape pass them by. His eyes traced the profile of her face and dropped down her neck. Something was there that hadn't been before. He stared at the brooch, struggling to push aside the pain that continued to fog his brain. Hadn't he taken that earlier? It had been upside-down then. And he'd kissed her .... The silver and enameled roses now clung to her dress right-side up. The light that had flickered in his chest before began to fill him.

"So, uh ...." he started, not sure how to bring up the subject that was now fully on his mind.

"Yes?" She smiled coyly at him.

"So, some night, huh?" He mentally kicked himself. *Real smooth there, Mick.* "What I mean is, um ... well, I'm sure tonight wasn't the way you always imagined you'd be proposed to, eh?" *Stupid, stupid, stupid!*

She smiled and laughed. "No, not quite. I mean, the first part was lovely, but really, you didn't need to arrange an attack to prove to me your manly prowess. I'm quite aware of it already."

Miguel chuckled, then groaned, grabbing his ribs at the stabbing pain. *You had to crack my ribs, too? But then again, at least I didn't get shot.*

"Are you sure you're all right?" she asked, half standing to move beside him again.

He waved her back. "As long as you keep talking, and quit making me laugh, it helps. It keeps my mind off the pain."

Maria sat back down. "My father also sent me with a message."

"And what is that, pray tell?" Miguel asked, his eyes twinkling despite his pain.

"I don't know that I shall tell you." Maria sat up all prim and proper.

"Can't you see I'm in pain? You should be kind and not make me guess." He would never not love the determined way she held herself.

"I didn't say I'd make you guess."

"Why won't you tell me then?" He gritted his teeth at a particularly bad jolt that sent a shock of pain through his knee.

"You didn't ask nicely enough."

"And how would you have me ask?"

"Be creative."

"Oh, fair lady, thou art cruel to ask so much of a man beaten, bruised, with a crushing headache this late at night and in such an unstable carriage."

Maria's laugh at his feigned despair was almost enough to ease the headache.

"Well, given that, I hardly think it is fair to keep such an ailing invalid in suspense. Just know that if we were not in a bouncing carriage, you would be expected to come up with something grand."

"Understood," he said gravely.

Maria smiled mischievously and looked at him through her lashes, suddenly serious and shy. "My father said to tell you that you have his blessing."

In the silence that followed, Maria looked away shyly from Miguel. Miguel rocked back as what she had said sank in, everything else swept away for the moment. Elated, he reached over to her and drew her beside him.

"And you?" he asked, raising her face up to look into her eyes.

"Yes, Miguel. A thousand times, yes." Miguel pulled her to him, crushing her against him. It was worth every stab of his ribs and pull of the stitches. She held him just as tight.

"I wish I could kiss you," Miguel whispered into her hair.

"Me too, but I don't think it would work too well with all the jostling," Maria replied. "There will be plenty of time later."

*Ready to follow Miguel and Maria into
a world of vampires, prophecy, and fate?*

DAUGHTER OF ZYANYA: BOOK 1
MORGAN J. MUIR

MARIA SETTLED down on a bench beneath a massive *roble de sabana*, its green branches shading the path, stark against the white stucco of the garden wall. Birds chattered and chirped in the foliage, unconcerned with her presence as Maria opened her well-worn book to a random page and began reading. After a time, the disconcerting feeling of being watched by unfriendly eyes pulled her from the pages. Looking up, she found Elisa, standing proud and arrogant, her blond hair pinned high on her head, glaring at her from across the garden.

They looked at each other for a long moment, a breeze whispering through the *roble*'s leaves.

"It's been a long time since you were here last," Maria said, finally breaking the silence.

"It hasn't changed much." Elisa's voice held a hint of disgust as she glanced across the garden.

Maria marked her place and closed the book. "I like it well enough."

"I'm sure you do, wrapped nice and snug in your little haven." Elisa walked around, feigning interest in the various plants and finding them horribly lacking.

Maria watched her quietly, noting that Elisa had dressed herself in the latest fashion, far too elegantly for the occasion, her dress cut almost to the point of impropriety.

"If it is so distasteful to you, why do you remain?" Maria said when Elisa snorted at her fourth plant. "Really, this aloof attitude does not become you."

"What does not become me," Elisa said, continuing her poised perusal of the flora, "is being forced into bad company."

"I do not see anyone holding a knife to your neck." Maria leaned to the side as though to look for a person behind Elisa. "Perhaps he is invisible?"

Elisa turned and looked down her nose at Maria, who remained on her bench, unruffled.

"What does not become me," Elisa said serenely, "is coming to congratulate a mestiza bastard girl on her engagement to some sea mongrel." She gave a small laugh as though she couldn't believe what she was about to say. "I am here for my father, who, for some absurd reason, feels an obligation to your father."

How dare she! Maria stood, grateful that she had the advantage in height. Schooling her face to calmness, she leveled her gaze at the girl before her.

"I know how highly you prize your standing in society, so I will not tell anyone of your gross breach of etiquette, not to mention your slanderous tongue." Maria allowed a note of disdain to enter her polite tone. "Perhaps you ought to go run to your father. I'm sure his presence will help to quell your childish impulses, and if his will not, no doubt your mother's can." She gave Elisa one last hard look and strode away.

The rich, wet scent of rain followed Maria to the house, along with the sound of the first heavy drops of rain hitting the orange tiles of the covered walkway. *Good,* she thought. *Let that wisp of a girl ruin her fine dress.* Elisa's words sat like a rock in her belly. What had she meant by it, calling Maria a mestiza? Maria knew she wasn't a bastard; it had been made clear to her at various times in her life that her parents had been married, but was it possible that she could, in fact, be of mixed blood?

Maria rubbed her hand against her dress, the cloth still damp in a spot from a moment of carelessness helping Nana. In an unexpected rush, she recalled all the times that servants seemed to have been extra-kind to her, treating her so much less formally than everyone else. She ran to her room, shut the door, and peered into the mirror to scrutinize her features.

Her eyes were still the same dark, rich brown they had always been, a color so deep that it was difficult to tell where the iris ended and the pupil began. Her hair, even darker than her eyes, waved gently down her back. Her high cheekbones gave a soft definition to her somewhat wide face, but nothing so different from any other Spaniard. Even her skin was rich olive color, darker certainly than Elisa and Betania's, but not unusually so for a Spaniard. She shook her head at her silliness and stepped back from her reflection.

"She was just trying to ruffle your feathers," Maria consoled herself.

"It looks like she succeeded." Maria spun around to see Nana standing quietly in the doorway. "What did she say to get you so upset?"

"Nothing worth repeating."

Nana snorted.

Maria gave a dismissive gesture. "She is upset about not getting Miguel and so she flung insults. She called me a mestiza and Miguel a sea mongrel. Calling Miguel a dog I'd expect, she's done that from the beginning, but calling me mestiza is a new low for her." She busied her hands in the silence that followed by straightening her dress and adjusting her mother's necklace.

"I see," was all the answer she got from the old woman.

After composing herself, Maria left the room, determined to finish her role as hostess as well as she could for the evening. The meal went smoothly, though Elisa remained cold and aloof. Maria noted with satisfaction the stains from the rain on Elisa's elaborate dress. Señor and Señora de la Cuesta were lively guests and spoke a great deal with their hosts about a range of topics, from past escapades of Sergio's and Ciro's lives as young traders to the current political climate and the growing tension with the natives. Maria found it fascinating, invigorating, and a little strange, since

Doña Olivia had never spoken with her as an adult before.

As the guests prepared to leave, there were more congratulations, and even Elisa condescended to offer terse felicitations. When the Diaz family had finally driven away and the doors were shut, Maria, Miguel, and Ciro sagged with exhaustion.

"I thought they'd never leave," Miguel joked, rubbing the back of his head. "My face hurts from smiling so much."

"You'd better work on those muscles, then," Maria laughed, nudging him. "I expect you to smile all the time."

"You're a hard taskmistress. Have mercy on me." Miguel pulled her close, and heat filled her face as he kissed her jaw.

"Shall we go to my study?" Ciro cut in, unperturbed.

Maria pushed away from Miguel but held his hand, following her father to his study.

"Well, it certainly was a pleasant evening," her father said as they passed through the study's door.

"Except for Elisa." Miguel shook his head, letting go of Maria and taking a seat on the couch. "She acted like she had mold in her dress or something."

"It would serve her right if she did," Maria said irritably, leaning against a mantle displaying several old revolvers.

"What do you mean?" Ciro settled himself into his favorite chair.

"She sought me out when they first got here so that she could tell me that the marriage of a mestiza girl and a sea mongrel was a waste of her time. She's changed lately, and I don't think it is for the better." Maria pushed away from the mantle and took a seat in a nearby chair.

Miguel snorted at the comment, but Ciro went very still, and Maria looked over at him curiously.

"What is it, Ciro?" Miguel asked quietly.

Her father heaved a sigh and walked to Maria.

"I should have told you about this long ago, *mi querida*," Ciro said sadly, kneeling next to Maria's chair. He touched the stone on her necklace, seeing things from long ago.

"Tell me what, Papa?" Maria asked softly, smoothing the wrinkles of his shirt across his shoulders.

"I loved your mother dearly. I first met her shortly after I'd broken with my first business partner."

"Gonza?" Miguel asked, and Ciro nodded.

"Our partnership failed over differing moral stances. I had a need to leave Maracaibo for a time, and a fellow, the son of a Spanish merchant himself, offered to take me along on his trading route. We stopped at his home, a Wayuu village, far to the north of here."

The knot in Maria's stomach tightened.

"And there, like an angel, was your mother. I loved her from the first time I saw her. She was very kind to me, helping me more than perhaps I deserved. As soon as we could, we married. Ayelen was an amazing woman. I'd always hoped to return there someday…"

"Why didn't you tell me?" Maria whispered, shaking her head in disbelief. "You let me believe…" *a lie.* How could he have lied to her for so long?

"What good would it have done?" Ciro hung his head and sat back on his heels. "The way the wealthy Spanish colonists treated Ayelen before I met her wounded her deeply, though she was far too proud to admit it. She had almost entirely given up her Spanish heritage by the time we met. She never wanted that for you, Maria, and I agreed. At best, you would have been treated no better by Society than they treat servants, but more likely they would have treated you worse for being my daughter. People are cruel, especially when they feel afraid."

"What would they have to be afraid of from me?"

Miguel gave her a thoughtful nod. "They feel they have dominance here by right of their birth. You would fly in the face of that. They would feel threatened, because if you could be in the upper circles of society, then why not their servants? They would see that their position is not as secure as they want to believe."

"You still should have told me." Bitterness constricting Maria's throat. "What else have you kept from me? Is my mother still alive somewhere?"

"Nothing, *mi querida,* nothing, I promise," Ciro said quickly. "As for your mother, I dearly wish she was—" His voice broke, and he returned to his chair, staring despondently into the fire.

"And what secrets do you keep from me that I ought to have known?" Maria turned her pain toward Miguel.

"I will tell you anything you ask." Miguel took her hand. She threw herself into his embrace, taking comfort in his strong arms. He spoke quietly to her while she rested her head against his chest. "I'm sure it was hard for your father to never openly speak of your mother. I think that if I ever lost you, I would do everything I could to keep your memory alive. However, I believe Ciro has been wise to keep this secret."

Maria pulled away a little to look at Miguel. "How could you think lying to me is a good thing?"

"You are to inherit all that he has, *mi morena*, and if it is found out that you are mestiza, not a full Spaniard, people will fight to rob you of what is yours. All that he has done, he has done for you."

Ciro roused from his reflections and looked at his daughter. "It is true, *hija*. After your mother died, you were my only direction, my only reason not to return to the sea and lose myself as quickly as I could. Perhaps, sometimes, I have even envied Vasco the ease of his escape after his wife died in childbirth, but I loved your mother too much. I loved *you* too much to run away like he did."

"I think it would be prudent to continue to keep this quiet," Miguel added. "I think so long as we don't make a fuss of it, any rumors Elisa starts will come across as nothing more than spite."

Maria looked into the fire. Perhaps they were right. It all felt too big for her to handle. She nodded her agreement. They understood better the intricacies of politics, and she didn't want to try to understand it all right now. They spent the rest of the evening quietly making plans for the wedding along with how to handle any further accusations. It was past midnight before they separated to go to their own rooms.

Maria flopped down onto her bed with a sigh, and Nana materialized out of the darkness.

"What a long day." Maria dragged herself to her feet and began undressing.

"Indeed," Nana said softly.

"I can't believe I never figured it out. Why couldn't you at least have told me?"

"I would have, but Ayelen asked me not to," Nana said, her voice unusually subdued.

"And you loved Ayelen more than me?"

Nana shook her head. "I have served the women of your family for a long time. Asking which I loved best would be like asking a mother which of her children she cherished more."

Maria thought a moment as she pulled off her dress. "Was it she who told you not to talk of her?"

"No, that was your father's request." Nana took the dress and handed Maria her night dress. "I only obeyed because it served Ayelen's wishes as well."

"Wishes? Besides hiding my heritage from me?"

"Ayelen was also of both worlds. Her mother was Wayuu and her father a Spaniard. He stayed with us in the village. He taught her and her twin brother the ways of the Spaniards, and to speak Castilian, alongside her mother, who taught them how to live as her people, the Wayuu. When they were old enough, she and her brother went with him to see the towns and live for a time among her father's people."

Maria sat on the side of the bed, her irritation forgotten, enraptured to hear the tale of her mother and grandparents.

"She was beautiful, talented, smart. Well-spoken and well-mannered. But whenever her or her father's peers learned she was mestiza, they would turn on her. She used to tell me that she could see it in their eyes the moment it happened, when their thoughts turned to disdain. She learned to rise above it, of course, but it always bothered her.

"There was one man, though, whose eyes never hardened against her. Despite many of the young men who sought her out among her mother's people, it was this Spanish merchant with whom she fell in love."

"My father!" Maria perked up in excitement.

"Your father, Ciro Álvarez Bosque." Nana nodded, sitting on the bed beside her. "His eyes would follow her everywhere. At first, she rebuffed him as insincere, but his persistence eventually won her over. 'It was his eyes,' she told me once. In his eyes, she could see that he never cared that she was anyone but Ayelen Zyanya."

"Zyanya?" Maria asked. "Not Cordova?"

"Your grandfather's name was Cordova. But by right, you are Maria Álvarez Zyanya."

"Zyanya," Maria repeated, trying the unfamiliar name on her tongue. "Does it mean anything?"

Nana gave Maria an appraising look. Just as Maria began to squirm under the scrutiny, Nana answered. "It means forever, or eternal. The women of your line have continued, unbroken, for a very long time. You are the firstborn daughter of a firstborn daughter whose mother, too, was a firstborn daughter, back generation upon generation."

Nana hesitated, took a deep breath, and continued. "Do you remember the story I told you, *hija*? The Wayuu legend of the Slaver and the Noble One?"

"Of course. I told it to Miguel and the girls once. He told us a story of a murderous, blood-sucking vampire called Arnold Paule in Europe. They dug up his grave and stabbed him with a stake, and then burned him for good measure." Maria smiled at the memory of the way Miguel had used the light of the bonfire to frighten and delight the girls as he'd told his gruesome tale.

"What do you remember of the Slaver and Noble One?" Nana prompted.

"It's the one where a strange, pale-skinned man appeared on the Wayuu shores centuries ago, with unnatural speed and strength. The Wayuu had been a peaceful people, and so they welcomed him, but he, in return, used his magic and enslaved the youth, hence the name of the Slaver."

"And the Noble One?"

Maria wondered what this had to do with anything, but her curiosity demanded she go along with it. "Some time later, another one of these creatures showed up, and this time the Wayuu were cautious, despite this man's claim of noble intentions."

"He claimed to be able to free us from the Slaver who had stolen so very much from our people already. When the elders had tried everything else they could think of and still failed to free themselves from the power of the Slaver, they turned to the noble one. He did as he said they would, but he was as they had originally feared, a trickster. The price he extracted from the Wayuu was even higher than the Slaver, but he kept his promise to help the Wayuu. To this day, they maintain their independence from all foreign invaders. This is why there have been two major rebellions against the colonists already." Maria picked at a bit of lint on her skirt. "Does Papa believe that tale? Is that why he thinks there will be another war?"

"That is the one, but I don't know if your father knows of it or not." Nana shook her head. "There is more to that tale than I have told you. Your mother knew, of course, but asked that I not say anything until you were ready."

"You think I'm old enough now?" Maria tried to swallow down the bitterness in the back of her throat. Even Nana kept things from her.

"I think there is no reason not to tell you, now that you know about your mother's family."

"Well, late though it is, today seems to be the day for telling me things." Maria tried to make light of the knowledge that, once again, important information had been hidden from her. *That's just the way it is. Everyone lie to Maria, she won't mind.*

Nana took both of Maria's hands into hers. "There is a prophecy connected to that tale."

Maria raised an eyebrow but didn't interrupt.

"It is said that one day a woman will arise who will free us from the continued servitude of the Noble One and the Slaver. One who will destroy those blood-sucking vipers who prey upon the hearts of our most vulnerable."

Irritation rose up in Maria. She was exhausted, and while being kept up later for tales of her mother was one thing, foolish ghost stories were quite another. "Why is this so important to tell me now? Why could it not have waited until the morning?"

"I'm telling you because you deserve to know. I'm telling you because the woman in the prophecy will be one of the Zyanya. She will be the last of the unbroken line. We will know her by her firstborn being a son."

Maria had had enough and pulled her hands gently from Nana's grasp. "And you believe this?"

"I'm certain of it."

AMARANTH DAWN
Available now on Amazon.com

Thank you for reading Aura of Dawn!

If you enjoyed reading Aura of Dawn, please consider leaving a review! It doesn't matter where—Amazon, Goodreads, Bookbub, or your own social media Reviews are like gold to an indie author, and they buoy my spirits and stoke the fires of creativity.

NEED MORE DAUGHTER OF ZYANYA?

You can find the rest of the series on Amazon

Aura of Dawn – a Prequel
Amaranth Dawn – Book 1
Aeonian Dreams – Book 2
Abiding Destiny – Book 3

ABOUT THE AUTHOR

Morgan J Muir fell in love with reading fantasy as child, and
could never get enough of it. She is a mom of
three crazy kids and lives in northern Utah.
You can find more of her stories
at morganjmuir.com

Made in the USA
Monee, IL
18 November 2023

46770559R00173